Baron Syndicate (-1): Crossroads of Destiny

By: Dennis L. Decker & Neil Miller

Cover illustration by:
Febrianto Pudi Utama

Printed in the United States of America

Revised edition

ISBN 978-0-9915595-1-0

mail@baronsyndicate.com

This book is dedicated to William Lanza, Jr., my programming teacher from high school. If it weren't for the group project he assigned to my class, the Baron Syndicate would not exist.

Chapter One

Baron Von Stupor was his name, or so he thought. His peers didn't care, as they were in the same predicament as him. The only difference is that this is his story, the story of a young man whose actions will affect the world around him more than he could ever know.

The Mason M. McFriendly Mental Wellness Center has been his home ever since reportedly causing an incident during his public disturbance hearing. Days come and days gone, he can only estimate his time spent there to roughly a year.

Baron Von Stupor (or Stupor for short) was in many ways an average person. He stood at an even six feet tall with a somewhat slender build, much like a runner who no longer runs.

His most peculiar feature by far was his mask, an enigmatic piece of headwear that has been firmly attached to his face for as almost long as he could remember. Its colors confused, its horns frightened, and the piercing stare of its large eyes discomforted nearly all who remained nearby it. To an average individual this would constitute a lonely experience growing up, but Stupor has come to terms with his curse and hence found some solace in his involuntary commission to the facility.

In the common room, Stupor found himself playing yet another round of checkers with a newer inmate known to him simply as Beeboo. The asylum was a place where on a lower level, identity had relatively no meaning. Many of the patients went by their birth name while others completely believed themselves to be someone—or something—else altogether. Beeboo was of the latter and Stupor found himself somewhere in-between, though unwilling.

Beeboo would be a remarkably average man if he were as old as he truly appeared. A scrawny frame, beady eyes, and a head full of peach fuzz did his image little justice. He showed ambiguous levels of intelligence that made his needs difficult to gauge, but if anything was obvious it was the man's love for losing at checkers.

It was the best of times, it was the worst of times. Checkers is fun! Stupor thought to himself while leaning back in his chair.

He casually stroked his chin with his thumb and examined the game board before him. He was overwhelming his lesser skilled opponent, yet taking an absurdly long time to figure his next move. He stared intently, disguising the fact that his thoughts were vastly distracted with unrelated miscellany.

If taking medicine with fruit juice can inhibit cancer-fighting agents, he contemplated, *then would it really matter if you're only treating a sinus infection?* "It makes no sense!" he spoke aloud, seemingly from nowhere.

Stupor's opponent looked at him curiously as Stupor, oblivious, concentrated on the board.

"You not make checker move again! Beeboo get sad!" grunted the man impatiently, his beady eyes squinting.

"My apologies!" spouted Stupor energetically, immediately jumping his opponent's final piece. "I win again, good sir!"

"Wow! You do a very good again!" Beeboo exclaimed, clapping his cheeks in shock.

"Oh, you always say that!" Stupor replied politely, dismissing the statement with a wave of his hand.

"We play again?" asked Beeboo excitedly.

"Well, I was hoping for something a little more action-packed, yes?" Beeboo didn't seem impressed, giving Stupor a grouchy frown. "Just think about it, Beep-boop!" Stupor pitched with vigor. "Ten epic pieces, 121 perilous holes, up to six possible players... the excitement of Chinese Checkers!"

Beeboo became oddly irate and flapped his arms erratically. "You listen to me! Beeboo name is Beeboo! Stop wrong! Now Beeboo want play checker again!"

"But you know, all we do is play checkers; it's been two days. Are you sure you're not interested in—"

"Wat?! Wat?! Wat?!" Beeboo grunted angrily, concerning nearby nurses.

"Oh, calm down. There's no reason to get—"

"B-but Beeboo want play checker!" the crazed patient wailed as he lunged at Stupor from across the small table.

Beeboo fell a bit short and clipped his knees on the table, sending checkers flying everywhere.

Stupor nimbly rose away from his chair as the table crashed to the floor with Beeboo's flopping body and flailing limbs.

The commotion caused a chain reaction with the other inmates, who began to get restless and panicked. Security guards and nurses swarmed into the room, calming people and apprehending both Beeboo and Stupor. Beeboo fought angrily while Stupor compliantly allowed himself to be restrained and forced to his knees.

He watched as Beeboo was sedated by the orderlies and carried out of the room. Shortly after, an official known to the inmates simply as Mr. Lanzendorf, came into the room and tapped his foot in irritation.

William Lanzendorf was the facility's security manager, enforcing the protection of life and property across the facility. He was a proud, clean shaven man who stood just above Stupor's height with his back straight and his nose high. He had short black hair coming to a point in the front like a duck's tail, creating a kite shape in tandem with his widow's peak. His attire was clean and neat, dressed in a formal hound's tooth business suit. The suit's dark color was contrasted by the shiny golden shield-shaped badge he wore on his chest. On the badge a balled up fist was depicted, surrounded by two olive branches with an eagle on top. Many wondered if his badge was official, though none have the gall to ask.

He approached Stupor and stared down at him with contempt. Stupor looked about the room and hardly noticed Lanzendorf's menacing vexation. He watched casually as the other guards gathered around him, obscuring his vision of the hospital staff.

Here we go again, he thought to himself.

"Starting fights yet again, B256?" Lanzendorf asked firmly.

Stupor's attention snapped to him. "Oh, not at all," he disagreed. "You see, Beeboo wanted to play checkers, and—"

"Be quiet!" Lanzendorf shouted abruptly.

"—we've been playing it for a couple days. Almost nonstop, you know!" Stupor continued, completely ignoring Lanzendorf's outburst. "So I simply—"

Stupor was unable to finish his sentence as Lanzendorf yanked him straight to his feet by his shirt. Lanzendorf pulled him in closer, trying to stare through the eyes of the mask and directly into Stupor's.

"If you keep doing that, you're going to tear my shirt," Stupor commented, unfazed. "It's my favorite one, you know!"

"Did you hear what I just said?" Lanzendorf asked, venom lacing every word. "I told you to be quiet. What does it mean when I tell you to be quiet?"

The two stared at each other for a moment. Stupor quickly became disinterested and began observing the room. Lanzendorf glowered with hatred. Noticing this, Stupor turned back to him and pointed his finger at him.

"Don't you look at me like that! That's rude!" he reprimanded. "I know you told me to shut up and I didn't hear you that time, so I apologize. But now when I do, you–"

Suddenly, Lanzendorf shoved Stupor against the wall, stunning him. He then leaned close into Stupor's face, staring a hole through the eyes of his mask.

"You know, I work hard to instill a sense of fear into all of these people," he said arrogantly. "It's their fear that regulates their behavior so I don't have to. Everyone in here knows what I can do to them. They keep in line because they know I'll do it, too. Why aren't you afraid like the rest of them? I know that behind that stupid mask of yours, you know it too."

Thinking for a moment, Stupor replied, "I guess after all this time I just forget to be scared. I mean, you've made so many threats, but you've never really followed through with–"

Stupor was cut off by an unexpected pain in his stomach as Lanzendorf rammed his fist into it. Stupor clutched his lower torso and doubled over as Lanzendorf stepped back, straightening his jacket sleeve.

"Watch yourself, you nut job," Lanzendorf spat. "Or I'll have you lobotomized before you know it."

Lanzendorf then dispersed the other guards before leaving the room. Stupor remained on the floor, not really caring to pick himself up. Under his mask, his eyes were sad.

***

"It's almost unnecessary for you to come by at all, with due respect," Lanzendorf boasted to Thaddeus Bark, the facility's human resources director. "Mr. Bark, this ship is being run as tight as ever with nary a crack nor leak to be found."

"Eloquent," replied the short, balding man. "However, standard procedure and all."

"Ha, ha. Standard indeed."

Lanzendorf gave a low, nearly undetectable chuckle as the two observed the common room. The only atmosphere present was the sunlight coming through the window, piercing the haze of fluorescent light. The inmates were peacefully mingling among themselves. Some were playing board games, just as Stupor and Beeboo engaged themselves again in checkers. Meanwhile, others merely sat by themselves to reflect on their inner person.

"It's just a matter of how you associate with these patients," Lanzendorf commented to Mr. Bark. "If you don't ensure they see you as a figure of authority, why would they ever respect you as one?"

"Of course," responded Mr. Bark. "But the other directors wonder about your perspective as far as how the patients are treated. You seem distrustful of every one of them."

Lanzendorf glanced at him skeptically and raised an eyebrow. "Sir, we can't forget that these patients are here for psychiatric reasons. Doesn't that make them rather unpredictable?"

"Just don't forget that this is an open unit. Many patients know why they're here. A few are even here voluntarily and aren't overly concerned with escaping."

"I would be more willing to believe that if it weren't for one troublemaker," Lanzendorf spoke loudly, shooting a glare in Stupor's direction.

Stupor, hearing Lanzendorf's words, waved at Mr. Bark energetically. The director returned a less than enthusiastic wave in response.

"I've read your reports on him," he affirmed, studying Stupor's mask. "I understand he seems to be a troublemaker, but while talking to me he's always been so polite."

"Because he's smart," Lanzendorf refuted, his eyebrow twitching. "He's too smart for his own good."

"Is that so?"

"He picks his battles. Who wouldn't be polite to us? We decide who goes and who stays, and he is very aware of that."

Mr. Bark glanced back at Lanzendorf, whose eyes have not yet left Stupor. "I hope by 'we' you mean the board of directors."

Lanzendorf's attention immediately darted back to Mr. Bark. "Absolutely, sir. By the way, I've taken the liberty of hiring an assistant for my day to day work."

Lanzendorf gestured toward a young man with a blank expression on his face sitting at a nearby table.

"You hired someone?" Mr. Bark asked. His demeanor was unimpressed and incredulous. "I was not made aware of this."

"I decided that it is imperative for me to have an assistant in order to maintain this facility at the security standards I have set," Lanzendorf explained, standing tall and firm.

"It also seems rather arbitrary," Mr. Bark commented with concern. "Mr. Lanzendorf, you already have one secretary and your personally trained security staff. When have you ever been in charge of selectively hiring anybody?"

"I apologize for the abruptness of this hire, but after you see the upward change in efficiency you'll realize this speedy decision was indeed for the best," Lanzendorf confidently explained. "His name is Ralph Higgins. He is dedicated to the simple commands he is given. He is very passive, very cooperative."

Mr. Bark gave a critical look to Ralph, who stared back in complete obliviousness. Ralph was just less than six feet tall with nothing worth any pride in his wardrobe. He wore faded, worn khakis with an orange unzipped runner's vest completely decorated in yellow highlighter strips. He had an average build, yet sported a double chin as if he had suddenly lost weight at some point. His hair was curly and matted, a brown color made darker from lack of regular bathing. His face was lightly peppered with acne and he had a noticeable unibrow that seemed to be kept eternally straight. The apathy that plagued his face was matched only by his inattentiveness to his own personal hygiene.

Ralph stared back at Mr. Bark for a moment before barely moving his lips at all to utter a long-winded, "Hello..."

Mr. Bark seemed less than impressed. He watched Ralph lethargically for a moment prior to noticing at his watch.

"I'll trust your judgment," he caved with a sigh. "But next time, please make sure that you hire employees through HR. We have protocols here. Not just facility procedure, but government-regulated processes that we are obligated to follow."

"Of course," Lanzendorf confirmed, standing erect with his hands clasped over his belt buckle.

"I have to go pick my kids up from school, so I suppose I will be on my way. I'm glad to see that everything is so swiftly back in order after yesterday's fandango."

"Oh man! You just said 'fandango'!" Stupor interjected, suddenly behind the two men. They turned and looked at him in surprise. "And I actually thought I was the only person in the world who used it in casual conversation!"

"Sit back down," Lanzendorf said to Stupor with excessive sternness.

"Mr. Bark, I was wondering something. Is 'fandango' just a word for a dance or is it an actual step?" Stupor asked, completely ignoring Lanzendorf.

Upset at Stupor's disregard for him, he drew in a breath to raise his voice but stopped himself when Mr. Bark spoke first.

"I'm afraid I only know it as a euphemism, son," he answered in a paternal tone. "I've never researched the word, but I do believe we have a dictionary here you could use to look it up."

Stupor stroked his chin for a moment and chirped, "I'mma look it up!" Giving a small wave, he then lightly jogged toward the bookshelves.

"Well, I suppose I'll be on my way then," Mr. Bark mentioned, turning his attention back to Lanzendorf. "When will you have those incident reports ready?"

"I'll have them sent before close of business tomorrow," Lanzendorf muttered, staring daggers at Stupor. "We're still talking to a few individual patients."

"Alright. You have a good evening."

Lanzendorf was silent and fixed his hateful gaze on Stupor as Mr. Bark left.

***

"Patient B256... we find ourselves here in my office yet again," Lanzendorf spoke pompously as he looked down his nose at Stupor. Calmly, he shut his door before returning to pace behind his desk. "You certainly are quite the magnet for trouble."

"Sure seems like it! I don't ask for trouble, but it certainly seems to follow me around," he answered, glancing inattentively about the room.

Stupor had always found Lanzendorf's office to be the most ornate room he had seen in the facility. He had special carpeting not found anywhere else in the building's management area as well as a tiny bookcase with a large trophy on it. It had a plaque on the front of its round wooden base with a crooked, leafless tree of gold grasping at the air. Like Lanzendorf's badge, Stupor had always pondered its legitimacy but could never get close enough to examine it. His desk was kept relatively simple, his office supplies precisely aligned with expert organization. His keyboard was kept covered by a small soft cloth. On his walls were a couple expensive paintings as well as certificates and awards Lanzendorf had obtained over the course of his security career. Just behind his desk was a large bay window, providing easy line of sight to the basketball court and common room entrance.

"Follow you? Kid, trouble doesn't just follow you; it emits from you like a stench! You have glaring issues with authority and this is obviously your way of 'sticking it to the man'. Why do you insist on making life so difficult for yourself?" Lanzendorf asked him with an eyebrow raised in scrutiny.

When Stupor failed to immediately respond, he gave his desk a ferocious slap. The sound of Lanzendorf's palm on wood reverberated about the room, startling Stupor and causing him to jump in his seat. Looking at Lanzendorf's desk,

Stupor noticed his office supplies now shaken out of place.

"What is authority?" Stupor mused in reply. "Is authority truly guidance, or just another form of oppression?"

"Authority is the regulation of people who are too stupid to regulate themselves properly," Lanzendorf answered gruffly, briefly breaking eye contact to fix his office supplies. "Authority is a firm necessity in this world, so that weak-minded simpletons like yourself don't destroy each other and then destroy themselves. Authority is peace and order. Authority is control. Authority is—"

Stupor chuckled, and Lanzendorf halted in mid-sentence to stare him down.

"Do you really think this is funny?" he asked Stupor, raising his voice. "Do you really think that making me waste my time to sit here and lecture you like a small child is amusing? I guess I'm not surprised, given your apparent lack of respect for anyone of stature."

"No, no, it's just that... Well, you're my authority. But you're not actually on the board of directors. That means you answer to them as your authority. But they answer to authority too, in the form of government regulation!" Stupor was by this point waving his hands in excitement. "And furthermore, all the countries of the world regulate each other via diplomacy! That makes us all too stupid to regulate ourselves!"

Lanzendorf blinked his eyes in confusion and asked him impatiently, "What is your point??"

"Basically, the joke is that you called yourself a dependent simpleton," he chirped in response.

Lanzendorf's eyes popped wide with surprise from Stupor's roundabout insult.

"I mean I know I'm taking what you said way out of context," Stupor backpedaled. "It was just a funny logic circle I thought about while you were going on about whatever."

"About whatever...?!" he uttered sharply with surprise.

Lanzendorf paced around for a few moments in complete silence, his face red like a fresh beet. Pursing his lips, he raised his balled up fists to slam on the desk when he looked down at his keyboard and back to Stupor.

"You're doing it again, aren't you?" he asked Stupor, jabbing his finger angrily. "You're doing it... again!"

"Doing what?"

"You know exactly what I'm talking about! You think you're so goddamn smart, don't you?!" Lanzendorf ranted, swinging his finger around in Stupor's face. "Get the hell out of my office! Get out!"

Stupor, heeding Lanzendorf's cue, rose out of his chair and quickly walked out of the room. On his exit, he immediately bumped into Guy Abernathy, Lanzendorf's Lead Officer.

"Your crew cut is quite short today! Good job with that!" Stupor complimented. "It makes your chin look a hundred times broader than it is, which is important if you wanna look manly."

Abernathy gave a somewhat grumpy look and lightly grabbed him by the arm. As he was being escorted, the two passed by the desk of Cheryl Green, Lanzendorf's secretary. She calmly looked up from her desk and curiously watched the two as they walked past.

"Did you do it again?" she apathetically asked Stupor.

Stupor chuckled in response, unable to slow himself due to Abernathy's forceful impatience. Meanwhile, Lanzendorf sat at his desk and called Cheryl on his office phone.

"How is everything, Mr. Lanzendorf?" she asked, lacking any form of enthusiasm.

"Cheryl, I want you to fill out a report for patient B256 regarding today's incident in the common room with patient B262. He gave very evasive answers to my questions and is passive-aggressively lashing out at authority. He provided no real reasons for starting the fight and I want you to forward the information to his psychiatrist for his next appointment."

"I'll take care of it, sir."

"Have it done in ten minutes."

"I'll do my best, sir."

"You're not paid for only your best, Cheryl."

"My apologies, sir."

Stupor arrived at a hall of isolation chambers just short of the building exit. Peeking into one of the tiny rooms through the door's window, he could only make out a simple bed and toilet. The room was slightly darker inside than the hall, the walls glowing with a lonely gray tint.

"Step inside, please," Officer Abernathy said to Stupor, ushering him toward the doorway.

"Do I really have to do solitary again?" Stupor asked him.

"You'll continue visiting solitary confinement until you fix your attitude problem." Abernathy impatiently nudged Stupor into the tiny room.

"But I feel fine!"

"Patient B262 isn't feeling well. He's been pretty ballistic ever since you slammed him on the table. Maybe when you start behaving better, you can spend less time in solitary."

"I feel like you're a little misinformed. I was playing check–"

"Whatever it says on paper is what happened. And personally, I don't have to take anything the patients say in here at face value, because all of you guys are crazy."

"What if we're sane and it's the asylum staff that's actually crazy?"

"Say that to the patient that got operated on because he wouldn't stop eating plastic spoons," Abernathy said, locking the door up tight and walking away.

"Well, that's different!" Stupor called to him as if he could be heard through the thick door.

Before long, Abernathy was completely out of sight. Stupor lay down on his hard bed and looked up at the fluorescent light lazily shining from up above.

I hate being in this room, Stupor thought to

himself. *Every time they put me in here, it reminds me of exactly where I am.*

***

"Morning starts, the sun so low,
Luminescence; feel the glow,
The brightness makes things hard to see,
Blindness gets the best of me,
Darkness now and deafness next,
As I fade I grow perplexed,

Someday your guard will fall.
And then you'll kill them all."

***

Stupor was startled awake by the sharp sound of the chamber door, unaware that he had even been sleeping. In the doorway stood a guard.

"I can come out already? Wait, was I asleep?" he asked, somewhat groggy.

"It's been a few hours, so you probably were," the guard replied.

"Hey, you're not Officer Abernathy," Stupor observed, failing to recognize the security guard's face. Looking at the badge, he could make out the name 'B. Herald'.

"Officer Abernathy is gone for the evening," the guard told him. "I'm here to escort you back to your chamber for lights out."

"Are you new here?"

"I normally do the morning shift."

"Ah! My isolation shifts are normally during the night, so I guess that's why I never see you!" Stupor chuckled.

Giving him a skeptical look, Herald ushered him out of the building and into the covered walkway. From there, they entered the facility's living quarters. The entire way, Stupor continued his friendly banter, seemingly oblivious to the guard's disinterest in Stupor's ramblings.

On entering his cell, Stupor saw his cellmate Jörg lying on the bottom of their shared bunk beds. He was still awake, but staring at the upper bunk's underside with a blank expression.

"Thank you for keeping us safe from roving bandits!" Stupor thanked Herald, who furrowed his brows in response, unsure of what to say.

The cell door was then appropriately locked and Herald out of sight.

Stupor clambered up to the top bunk and lay down, looking at the ceiling.

"I bet the underside of this bunk is more interesting than the ceiling, eh, buddy?"

"Nur die Insekten," Jörg replied, his hard stare concentrated and unbroken.

Jörg was an interesting individual who has been living in the asylum for longer than Stupor. He regularly showed the ability to understand English, yet as far as anyone remembered he has only spoken German. The two boasted a sort of pseudo-friendship that no one could really know the true nature of. Jörg was tall and slender with scruffy black hair. Contrary to popular belief, he dressed in medical scrubs by choice.

"I think that for a perfectly healthy person, if you can't even recall to the day how long you've been here, then you shouldn't have to stay here anymore," Stupor lamented. "I think it's been around a year, but I don't even know anymore."

"Sie werden mich niemals gehen lassen. Das ist wahrscheinlich eine kluge Entscheidung."

"It probably wouldn't be so bad if I weren't so... bored here. I mean, board games are always awesome and I'm quite proud of my greenhouse-grown potatoes, but... is that all there is for me here? Sitting in this tiny room, writing on this tiny desk? Checkers with Beeboo every day? Jörg, tell me honestly... am I really crazy? Do I really belong here?"

"Alle Menschen sind Monster," Jörg said, briefly poking his head out and smirking. "Die Patienten hier haben das akzeptiert. Ich denke, du bist genauso verrückt wie jeder andere. Ich glaube nicht, dass du hierher gehörst, weil du nicht akzeptierst, was du bist. Das ist eine Schande, denn ich respektiere dich. Es ist selten, dass ich ein anderes menschliches Wesen respektiere."

Stupor remained silent for a moment before saying with a thumbs up, "That certainly sounded like optimism, so thank you. I really appreciate your support for me!"

"Du bist ein Narr auf deine ganz besondere Weise."

Stupor, feeling sleepy again, lay down and closed his eyes. Enveloped by the dim moonlight that lit the room, he finally began to dream.

***

"You won't be there for long, son. Just be honest–and for God's sake, don't fake anything! None of that 'potatoes saving the world' baloney!"

"You're gonna be just fine, sweetie... Please, try to get better. We'll come visit when we can, we promise!"

Chapter Two

"Wow!" Stupor cried, bolting upright in his bed. His roommate glanced at him from the nearby desk. "Jörg! I was thinking about my parents and next thing I know I had the craziest dream! I got attacked by two fat guys in an alley because they thought the two tons of cocaine I was smuggling was powdered sugar! They ate it all, man!"

"Ich vermisse die alten Zeiten als Drogenbaron..." Jörg replied with furrowed brows.

"Yeah, something like that. Hey, remind me to record this in my dream diary too, whenever I finally get that old thing started. I gotta think about my family before bed more!"

"Ich hoffe, dass ich dich eines Tages in deinen Träumen verfolgen kann. Ich klopf auf Holz!" Jörg mentioned while smiling brightly and knocking on the wooden desk.

Stupor hopped out of bed and navigated his way to the dresser. Opening it up, he extracted a clean orange shirt identical to his current dirty shirt and began getting dressed while Jörg looked the other way.

"You down for some Shashki?" Stupor asked his roommate.

"Russische Dame? Niemals, ich spiele nur durch und durch amerikanische Spiele!"

"I heard someone talking about it the other day. I think it's for lunch! I'll check for it on the menu. Are you coming, too?"

"Ich kann nicht. Ich bin damit beschäftigt über die anderen Patienten zu fantasieren. Vielleicht später, ich habe mein Soll noch nicht erfüllt."

Stupor examined Jörg's face for a moment and said, "You don't seem too interested, so I'm just gonna go now. I wanna make sure I have breakfast before medicine time! Ciao for now, buddy!"

"Wenn du in Amerika leben wirst, könntest du zumindest Englisch sprechen," Jörg grumbled as Stupor performed an exaggerated waddle out the door and into the hallway.

As Stupor wobbled and bobbled he held his arms to either side of him, uttering "Blub, blub, blub," with every step. On the bottom floor, he happened to notice Ralph watching him blankly in passing. Stupor stopped and stared right back at the young man.

"You know why I do that?" Stupor asked him after a few moments.

"Nope..." Ralph mumbled with hardly any enunciation.

"It reminds me of how I'll have to walk if I don't exercise daily and eat healthy! You should try it too. It's very enlightening!"

Ralph, rather than responding, continued to stare at Stupor while swaying ever slightly. Stupor continued to stare back, mimicking Ralph. After a few moments, Ralph cracked an immeasurably slight smile.

"You're funny," he breathily complimented.

Suddenly, the awkward moment was broken by the sharp sound of Lanzendorf shouting for Ralph through his two-way radio. Ralph slowly looked over his shoulder toward the building exit and then back to Stupor.

"I gotta go now," he uttered prior to shuffling away.

Shrugging, Stupor followed him out of the living quarters and then cut across the courtyard to the common room. The weather was very nice; the temperature moderate, a calm early summer breeze blowing. The sky looked friendly and inviting, with billowing clouds scattered about.

Stupor noticed a few inmates practicing shots on the basketball court near the common room. Elsewhere, he saw other patients kicking a soccer ball around. Stupor gave them friendly waves as he passed, but none appeared to notice his effort. Without caring, he continued to the common room. Upon entering, he noticed something very different about the atmosphere.

There's a lot more security in here than normal, he thought to himself. *I know that's not because of yesterday.*

He observed the guards staring intently in the general direction of the room's corner. Following their gaze, he saw a very large man sitting at a faraway table. Stupor could not gauge his height, but noticed that he barely fit the chair in which he was sitting. He appeared muscle bound from head to toe. His medical scrubs barely fit him, the constricting sleeves defiantly torn off. The unique indentifier on the back of his shirt was C26 in large, printed characters. His head was completely bald and he maintained a horrible, unfriendly scowl. He sat completely upright, his arms crossed, and stared out a nearby window.

I've gotta meet this guy! Stupor thought eagerly to himself.

He then strolled straight over to patient C26 and waved energetically. C26 slowly turned his gaze toward Stupor.

"Hi!" Stupor chirped.

The frowning patient simply returned his gaze to the window.

"What's your name?" Stupor asked.

"Go away," C26 gruffly answered.

"No, it's not."

C26 winced briefly before he returned his grumpy stare to Stupor. "Go away," he repeated, overpronouncing each word.

"Oh, come on. I'm not that dumb," Stupor fearlessly continued, holding his hand out in a friendly gesture. "Nice to meet you! My name is Baron Von Stupor!"

On hearing Stupor's name, C26's impatience immediately turned into mild confusion.

"What kind of a ridiculous name is that?" he sardonically asked.

"Unorthodox and superbly creative!" Stupor responded with vigor, spreading his arms wide.

"Feh," C26 spat with disgust, leaning forward and propping his head on one arm. "This is an asylum, so you must have given that stupid name to yourself. Now go away." C26 waved his hand dismissively and returned his gaze to the window.

"You know what?" Stupor asked, leaning on the back of a chair with his hands. "I bet you just need a really good friend to warm up to, Mr. C26! And you know, I'm really good at—"

"Stop!" C26 ordered sharply, cutting Stupor off. He stood straight up and glowered down at Stupor who had by now returned to an upright position with his arms hanging to either side.

"Holy crap, you're huge!" Stupor exclaimed, estimating his height at around seven and a half feet.

"Stop using those contractions around me! Do you not care about your own language?" C26 asked him angrily.

"Well, of course I care!" Stupor responded as he matter-of-factly stuck his finger in the air. "'tis the very foundation of man's communication of information in this great nation!" Stupor then chuckled and added, "I threw that last part in there for *m-m-m-maximum*—"

"If you care so much, then why must you butcher it with shortcuts such as contractions?" C26 asked aggressively, cutting Stupor off.

"Contractions are very much accepted in the English language by scholars all over!"

"Yes, Terran scholars. Barbaric, uncivilized scholars with no sense of pride in their language. Scholars who accept anything that communicates their messages, cutting all corners and taking any sense of grace out of their speech."

"Terran? Are you an alien or something?"

"You would neither understand nor believe me; no one here does. Now leave me alone, you whelp."

"Are you crazy? You're the coolest person I've spoken to in a long time! I–"

"Damn you, obnoxious Terran!" C26 swore loudly. "Stop using contractions!"

Stupor and C26 stared at each other for a few moments in silence. Stupor raised his finger to say something, but was unexpectedly shoved backward by the looming giant. Stupor tried to catch himself, but was too surprised by the force of the push and wound up falling over a table and off the other side, becoming tangled between a couple chairs.

"Go away!" C26 ordered sternly as a couple nurses came to assist Stupor.

"Patient C26, come with us!" ordered Officer Abernathy, approaching the man.

"I will obey no one unless I am defeated in honorable battle!" he spat back in defiance.

Abernathy stopped long before reaching him, allowing the other guards to catch up.

"Sir, you need to calm down and come with us," he commanded once more.

"You do what people say if they beat you up?" Stupor asked C26, now back on his feet.

"If I can be defeated in honorable combat, then I am bound by my honor to serve the one who defeated me. However, I could challenge every Terran here, one by one, to unaugmented combat and emerge victorious. Unfortunately, none of you scum will accept my challenge; instead you choose to hide behind your meager tranquilizers and hold me here like a caged animal! All of you are the very definition of cowardice and shame!"

"Patient C26, this is your final warning!" Abernathy spoke, backpedaling to the guards that had followed him. "Come with us peacefully or we will restrain you and take you by force! I have a stun baton and I will use it!"

"I will not follow your orders until you come forward and defeat me, pathetic Terran stravag!"

As C26 finished his sentence he slammed his arm down on the table, smashing it cleanly in half. The guards then quickly approached him with stun batons in hand, Abernathy electing to stay behind and shout orders. Orderlies swarmed into the room, tranquilizer at the ready.

One guard approached C26 and swung his baton, but his wrist was quickly grabbed by C26. With his free hand, the giant then landed a haymaker into the security guard's face, dropping him instantly. As he turned around, a second guard managed a glancing blow with his stun baton on C26's shoulder, causing him to recoil backward. C26 kicked the guard away and swung his arm 180 degrees, clubbing a third to the ground. C26 quickly turned back around and grabbed the prior guard's own stun baton. The guard seized violently as C26 firmly pressed it against his neck.

The colossal man shoved the guard away, but was piled on by three other guards, all stunning him at the same time. C26's flailing was by this point disorganized and the guards quickly forced him to the ground long enough to fasten zip ties around his hands and feet. Orderlies then closed in and injected the man with sedative medicines, rendering him barely conscious. The remaining unhurt guards carried C26 out of the room while Abernathy, looking rattled, stayed behind with the orderlies.

The inmates watched the scene unfold in an awkward silence. As soon as patient C26 was out of sight, Stupor exploded with enthusiasm.

"Whoa man, wasn't that the coolest thing ever?!" he squealed, his arms waving erratically.

"Oh ya! He do really good!" he heard Beeboo speak from elsewhere in the room. "You want play checker now?"

***

After checking in, Stupor strolled into the office of Dr. Walter Goodrich, lead psychiatrist and board director.

"Hello, Dr. Goodrich! Pleasant day, isn't it?" Stupor asked with a bounce in his step.

Dr. Goodrich was an older African-American gentleman. He was a bit stout, similar in size to Mr. Bark, though with a full head of steadily graying hair. Dr. Goodrich sat behind his desk and awkwardly pulled himself forward, verifying the height setting of his office chair en route.

Dr. Goodrich's office was particularly blue, if nothing else. Stupor found himself blinded by the brightness of the paint job, and the redwood desk was so old, faded, and decrepit that Stupor had even taken to referring to it as 'deadwood'. The office in every other way was kept very tidy and often smelled of pine due to his automatic air freshener.

"You're particularly excited today," observed Dr. Goodrich, noticing Stupor's energetic strides to his seat.

"Oh, today is very exciting!" spouted Stupor, glowing with enthusiasm. "We got a new patient and that guy is big and strong, I tell you!"

"Oh yes, I heard about that about a half hour ago. You were antagonizing him, weren't you?"

"Pshaw, no! I was trying to make friends! I think he's warming up to me; he just needs a little time to get acclimated to his friendly new surroundings!"

"That may well be the last time you get to see him."

"No way! He'll be back, you'll see."

"I suppose we'll find out later, as I expect there emergency board meeting regarding him."

"I hope he stays! I'm still excited from how cool that was!"

Dr. Goodrich picked up a paper on his desk and looked it over.

"Well, I'd like to get down to business if you don't mind," said the doctor without looking up.

"I would actually like to start with discussing the events that transpired yesterday between yourself and Beeboo."

"Oh, that. Well, Booby likes to play checkers, yep!"

"Is that all you have to say on the matter?" asked Dr. Goodrich, furrowing his brows.

"I think he likes to lose!"

"So what's this about slamming Beeboo onto the table after the game?"

Stupor tapped his chin and asked, "Now why would I do a silly thing like that? It's a known fact that I won the game."

"To be fair, this wouldn't be the first time you've attacked someone unprovoked. We can't forget the fact of why you're here in the first place."

Stupor put his hands on his hips, offended. "Hey now, that's not fair!" he defended. "I'm not trying to say the whole courtroom incident didn't happen; I just wasn't there!"

"I don't mean to assert that you're guilty or innocent, I'm just saying that someone attacked the magistrate during your trial and that we have the eye witness testimonies of a great number of people saying that a man in a mask that looks exactly like yours did it."

"Exactly, you say? That's a pretty tough pill to swallow."

Waving his hand dismissively, Dr. Goodrich stated, "We're getting off-topic. How did Beeboo get slammed into the table? According to the incident report, you caused that to happen."

"Those reports are just opinions on paper!"

"You're being evasive as always," the doctor observed skeptically. He sifted through Stupor's file and extracted a new piece of paper. Grabbing a pen, he looked at Stupor. "Let's talk about your name now."

Stupor blankly stared for a moment before happily claiming, "I'm Baron Von Stupor!" He gave the doctor a friendly wave.

"No, not that. I'd like you to tell me why you refuse to use or even hear your birth name."

Stupor's shoulders slumped. "Because it's not my name."

"Despite your birth records?"

"Yep! Despite everything!"

"What if there is a way I could prove to you your true identity?"

"Is there a way?"

"How would you react if I could show you empirical proof that you are not actually Baron Von Stupor?"

Stupor sat back in his chair and stroked his chin. "Idunno, I've never really thought about that before. I suppose it would be pretty cool."

Raising his eyebrows, Dr. Goodrich asked, "You think it would be 'cool' if I were to shatter everything you think about your identity?"

"Well yeah! I think it would be interesting to be proven wrong sometimes, especially about something like that. It'd be epic, too! Just like in a movie!"

"Why would you enjoy being proven wrong?"

Stupor leaned forward and rested his elbow on the doctor's desk. "It keeps things interesting. Don't you ever get bored sitting there thinking you're right all the time?"

"There's no need for personal attacks on me; I'm trying to help you."

"Seems more like you're getting in my way. But hey, I'm sorry if I hurt your feelings. You're pretty sensitive for a psychiatrist."

"I'm getting in your way? How so?"

"Well how else am I going to go get lunch if you keep bringing me in here and claiming I'm not who I claim to be? I mean, I'm way more interested in the country fried steak than sitting here and playing the Same Lame Name Blame Game with you."

Before Dr. Goodrich could respond, Stupor began chuckling at his own joke. Dr. Goodrich let him finish his laughing, unimpressed. Stupor added, "The 'Same' part didn't really belong, but I threw it in there for *m-m-m-maximum rhymage!*"

Dr. Goodrich let out an exasperated sigh and said, "Let's just get one more thing out of the way and I'll go ahead and let you go."

"Sure thing!"

"Your name. How did you get it?"

"Ah, 'tis a tale of old!" said Stupor, drawing in a breath. Then without pausing, he quickly spoke his story. "It all started back during the big Video Game Crash of nineteen sixty-whatever.

"The magical guardian entity Guitari was still

recovering from a harsh defeat at the hands of an extraterrestrial cartridge monster that ate out the guts of many people! The spirit king Pretendo emerged from the rubble of a collapsed building and in Guitari's wake created a new industry in her image! No wait, Pretendo was a... guy? Eh, it doesn't matter.

"Anyway, and that's about when my parents were born. One thing led to another, and then my parents lost a bet against Guitari, and thusly agreed to name me Baron Von Stupor. And then everyone went out for bagels. The end!"

After scribbling notes on a piece of paper, Dr. Goodrich then asked, "And we all know that in nobility, the letter V in 'von' does not actually get capitalized. Why is it capitalized in yours?"

Leaning forward, Stupor whispered, "You never heard this from me, but Guitari theorized that a capital V would increase my strength by fifty percent. But personally, I don't see any way to prove that."

"Mm-hmm. Well, I suppose that's enough for today. Could you please speak to Michala at the desk to schedule your next appointment?"

"Oh, certainly! I do enjoy our talks," Stupor complimented while standing up to shake Dr. Goodrich's hand.

"I bet you do. I'll see you at group therapy tonight, Mr. Stupor."

"Oh, you bet!"

***

In the common room sat Steve Jenkins, the financial director and yet another member of the board of directors. He dressed in a formal dark gray pinstripe business suit and kept his neat auburn hair parted in the middle.

He took a moment from his meal to look up and noticed Lanzendorf approaching, holding a tray in hand.

"William Lanzendorf, how are you today?" he greeted as the security manager sat down on the same side of the table as him, not far down.

"Lunchroom food," Lanzendorf responded with a snarl. "If it weren't free, I could bring a TV dinner to work every day and the job would be just as done."

"I don't think it's that bad."

"Being the financial director, it'd be foolish to think otherwise. God forbid if you deliberately made a poor financial decision."

"Hardy har. Shouldn't you be off somewhere waking up your staff or pulling donuts out of their mouths?"

Lanzendorf chuckled and bit into his country fried steak he fashioned into a sandwich using a hamburger bun. As he chewed, he surveyed the room suspiciously. As if on cue, Stupor trotted in and went to the tray pick-up window to receive his food.

"There he is," Lanzendorf said out loud. "It's like I can feel that little idiot coming."

"Who, that guy?" asked Mr. Jenkins, pointing

toward Stupor.

"Yeah."

"What's your problem with him again?"

"He's too big for his britches. He thinks he's smart and acts like he runs the place. He enjoys being a pain in my ass."

"Huh. You can't let it bother you, though," Mr. Jenkins mentioned, wiping his mouth with a napkin. "You probably know well enough that in a position like yours it's way too easy to get in trouble."

"It's only easy to get in trouble if you don't know what you're doing. As long as you follow standard procedure and keep everyone in check, everything stays nice and balanced." Lanzendorf rebutted. "That boy there is the odd weight; he doesn't stay in check."

"Why does he wear that mask? The facility normally makes people take that stuff off."

"According to Dr. Perez, he has some stupid medical note that says it's impossible to remove without surgery. That means that legally we can't require him to take it off."

"Isn't it necessary to remove it, then?" Mr. Jenkins asked before taking another bite of his sandwich. "Like, medically necessary?"

"He can do everything from eating to bathing without taking it off. Unless he agrees to surgery, that mask stays put."

"That medical note sounds bogus. Have you tried pulling the mask off?"

"Nope. Too much risk if the other directors

find out. I'd love to debunk that note, though," Lanzendorf muttered, neglecting his lunch. "Dr. Goodrich even thinks he's faking his insanity."

Mr. Jenkins, surprised, set his drink down quickly before he could take a sip. "Oh yeah? We have a case of malingering on our hands?"

"Possibly. It could connect the dots on why he's so different from all the other inmates. Let's just say I wouldn't be surprised if our little friend turned out to be a lying manipulator, on top of everything else I despise about him."

"Sounds like you've got a grudge, Bill."

"I don't have a grudge against individuals, just against insubordination and disrespect."

"Well, just keep it professional, huh? As it stands, the other directors are uncomfortable with the way you view the other inmates, even though the facility gets spectacular reviews."

Lanzendorf looked at Mr. Jenkins with an eyebrow raised. "Don't act special," he shot in reply. "You feel the same way I do about them, so don't try to give me advice on how I should view these people."

"Bill, I don't like them any more than you do, that's absolutely correct. But for starters, it's not common knowledge. You're the only person I actually talk to on a personal level around here. Secondly, I repeat: just keep it professional. You bring results—very good results—and that's a great leverage for you as far as the board is concerned, let alone Thaddeus.

"However, I don't know how you do your

job, I don't want to know how you do your job, and personally I don't care how you do your job. Ever since that kid got here, the board has been noticing you acting weird around the inmates. If this kid is upsetting the balance you're talking about, you may need to just let him do it and allow procedure to take care of him."

"Steve," Lanzendorf said with a fierce stare. "I appreciate that you care, but why don't you take care of your job as a *financial director* and let me handle disciplinary issues in this facility?"

Mr. Jenkins stared back at Lanzendorf for a few moments and then rolled his eyes.

"Whatever, Bill," he resigned, standing with a low chuckle. "I'm just saying, that's all."

Lanzendorf watched as Mr. Jenkins returned his tray. Suddenly, he was startled when he heard a loud sneeze from behind him. Turning quickly, he found himself staring straight into the wide, vacant eyes of Stupor's mask.

"Sorry about that, Mr. Lanzendorf," Stupor apologized. "Say, do you mind if I call you Bill?"

Lanzendorf stared at him hard without saying a word.

"I tell you what," Stupor mentioned. "I was originally going to ask for a napkin since I just sneezed all over my mask, but I can see you're clearly busy with your meal. I'll just get my own."

Stupor ambled away toward tray pick-up and Lanzendorf resumed eating his meal.

***

“Alright everyone, please come in and have a seat,” Dr. Goodrich asked the group of patients entering the room.

The patients hardly acknowledged him as they moved to random chairs, arranged to form a circle. Stupor plopped into his chair and began twiddling his thumbs. To one side sat Jörg.

The room was very inviting, with a small fireplace on one side with a gas fire producing a dim, friendly light. The walls had fine copies of paintings along with a board featuring some select crafts created by patients in the past.

“Beeboo has been moved to our morning sessions, so he will not be joining us. Instead, we will now be welcoming a new patient, Marcus Johnson,” continued Dr. Goodrich, ushering in a middle-aged African-American man.

Marcus moved over toward Stupor and stood behind the chair adjacent to him.

As Dr. Goodrich continued talking, Stupor observed Marcus. He seemed to be of an average build, wearing simple clothes consisting of a pair of black cargo pants and a gray t-shirt with a music artist he could not identify on it.

“Would you like to sit?” Stupor asked the man, gesturing toward the chair Marcus leaned upon. Marcus seemed confused.

“Sit? What are you talking about?” he asked in reply.

“In the chair. You’re welcome to sit down if you want.”

"A chair? I have no idea what that is."

Stupor suddenly fell out of his chair, agape. Marcus stared back uncomfortably.

"What monster hid the marvelousness that is the chair from this poor man?!" Stupor ranted as he rose to his feet. "I demand answers!"

Dr. Goodrich gently placed his hand on his face and massaged his cheekbones in frustration. Looking to Marcus, he asked, "Do you mind if I tell them?"

"I don't mind," he responded with a mildly confused look.

Dr. Goodrich spoke to the group, "As Mr. Stupor is now painfully aware, Marcus has visual agnosia. His specific ailment is that he has lost all concepts of chairs and their function. If you show him a chair, he will not recognize it. If you explain it to him, he will not understand. He is very uncomfortable being sat in a chair, or most anywhere.

"Needless to say, Mr. Johnson is welcome to stand during our sessions and his treatment until he is comfortable enough to sit down voluntarily. Therefore, Mr. Stupor, there should be no other reasons to disrupt our sessions and embarrass the patients. Are we clear?"

"Oh..." Stupor uttered, slightly embarrassed. "My apologies, dear sir. Rest assured that we will do everything we can to—"

"Sit down, Stupor!" a female inmate chided. "Stop wasting everyone's time."

Stupor turned and looked at the inmate,

Jocelyn Baxter. Jocelyn is a relatively new patient, and a 19-year-old pathological liar. She dresses in medical scrubs, her light brown hair draped over her shoulder and hanging in front of her chest. She had relatively cute facial features that were often hidden by her frequent frowning.

Stupor turned back to Marcus and shot him a quick thumbs-up before sitting down. After a brief moment of silence, Dr. Goodrich picked up a small stack of rectangular paper scraps bound together by a rubber band. He then unbound them and began passing out a single scrap and a pen to each patient.

"So today we're going to start off with a new group exercise I read about, called Mimic," Dr. Goodrich announced to the group of inmates that sat before him. He then faced Marcus. "Mr. Johnson, in our group therapy sessions we play a simple game in the beginning. This is just to have a little fun and lighten the mood before we get to the actual therapy session."

Marcus nodded and accepted the paper and pen. Stupor held his paper and pen in his hand and stroked his chin as Dr. Goodrich continued his explanation.

"We are first going to write the name of a famous celebrity on your papers, and—"

"Do they absolutely have to be celebrities?" Stupor asked, cutting him off.

"Technically yes, but as long as it's a name that everyone in the room recognizes, that's fine too. And after everyone is done, we need to put all of the papers into a hat and we'll take turns drawing them. Whatever name we draw, we'll do an imitation of the celebrity we drew. Afterward, we'll try to guess who the celebrity was."

After a few minutes, the papers returned to Dr. Goodrich and he placed them inside of a top hat he had brought with him.

Shaking the hat and stirring the scraps, he said to the group with a smile, "Alright, we're all set. Would anyone like to go first?"

Stupor's hand shot up while all other hands stayed down. Dr. Goodrich sat quietly for a few moments, ignoring Stupor. Giving up, he stood up and shuffled his hand inside the hat.

"Actually, I have a great idea," he said to everyone. "I understand not many of you may be so comfortable right away, so I'll go first."

He pulled a name out of the hat and nodded his head. He then stepped to the center of the circle and clasped his hands over his belt buckle.

"This one should be easy for you all," the doctor said with a light smirk. He glared over everyone's heads and said with terrible acting, "You've got to ask yourself one question: 'Do I feel lucky?' Well do ya, punk?"

Some of the inmates laughed at the doctor as he stood, smiling. Stupor found himself in deep thought wondering where he had heard that phrase before.

"It's okay," he said. "I'm just a doctor, not an actor. But that's exactly the purpose here; we're supposed to laugh and have fun. We need to feel comfortable. So, can anyone guess who I am?"

"Jim Carrey!" Stupor burst, sticking his finger in the air.

Before Dr. Goodrich could respond, another inmate spoke out in a high-pitched voice, "Are you serious? Jim Carrey?"

Stupor easily recognized the voice as that of Terry Rogers, a 31-year-old man diagnosed with schizophrenia shortly after the loss of his wife. Also suffering from dwarfism, he sat with his feet barely hanging off his chair, dressed in medical scrubs that were specially tailored to fit him.

"Jim Carrey totally said that!" he shot back at Terry.

"You don't have any respect for classics, do you? It was Clint Eastwood, you doofus!"

"Oh no, Jim Carrey said it, too. In that one movie!"

"You don't even know which one?!"

The other patients began to grow restless. A few began to mumble to each other and others to no one in particular.

"Ladies and gentlemen, please calm down!" Dr. Goodrich demanded, exasperated.

Everyone quickly became quiet.

"Mr. Stupor is technically correct; Jim Carrey did say it in 'The Mask'," the doctor confirmed. "However, the name written on my paper was Clint Eastwood. Mr. Stupor and Mr. Rogers were both correct. Come on now, this is supposed to be fun. Let's try to relax and not take offense to things as trivial as that. Are there any volunteers for the next paper?"

No hands were raised. Terry pouted in his chair and Marcus shuffled his feet awkwardly. Stupor was preoccupied, watching the fire in the fireplace behind him.

"Stupor, didn't you have your hand raised earlier?" asked the doctor. Stupor whipped back around to face him.

"I suppose I could," Stupor said reluctantly. "...As long as everyone is willing to smile!" He finished his sentence with a swing of his arm and reached deep into the hat. Pulling a paper out, he bounced with excitement and stepped to the center of the circle.

"You guys will never get this one!" he glowed. He then pulled his feet close to each other, stiffly straightened his back, and looked at the ceiling.

Stupor then slowly marched about the circle, looking individual inmates. "You are all scum!" he spat in a mocking tone. "Do you know why? Because I have power and you have none! I love pushing you around! I get to do whatever I want and my bosses all look the other way! I make threats and I physically abuse people! How do I get away with it? My victims are all crazy! Nobody will ever listen to them!"

Everyone sat in confusion for a moment as Stupor looked around.

"...And I have a huge nose!" he continued, pointing at his mask.

Terry immediately said aloud, "Hey, all that sounds just like Lanzendorf."

Before Dr. Goodrich could correct him, a cacophony of laughter erupted from the patients. Stupor excitedly hopped around, cheering and pointing at his scrap of paper. The doctor simply stared forward, a flat expression across his face. Noticing Stupor in front of him, he looked up to meet his gaze.

"That's how you have fun!" Stupor gleamed, shooting him a thumbs-up.

Dr. Goodrich stared back quietly in response.

***

Stupor and Jörg arrived at their cell at the same time. Jörg looked at Stupor and chuckled, shaking his head.

"What's so funny?" Stupor asked him as he crawled into his bottom bunk.

"Lanzendorf," Jörg replied with a very thick accent. He was still smiling from ear to ear.

"Oh, you have no idea! I've been writing his name on those paper scraps for months now, and this is the first time it's ever paid off, ever! I'm quite proud!"

"Ich habe schon seit langer Zeit nicht mehr so gelacht!"

"I do feel bad about Dr. Goodrich, though," Stupor admitted as he sat down in a chair. "He really tries hard to help the patients. Idunno, do you think I'm selfish for having fun during our sessions?"

"Der Mann macht seinen Job, aber nur sehr

schlecht. Er könnte so viel mehr erreichen, wenn er einer von uns wäre, anstatt ein Beobachter."

"It's just that life here is so boring! I mean I know I say that a lot, but I can't get over it! Day in day out, same old same old. I used to believe my parents when they told me I really needed to get better to leave the asylum. I cooperated, but nothing changed about me, about how I felt, or about how I'm treated by others. Months later, no change. What's the point? I don't feel any better, and in fact I still feel perfectly fine! Just as fine as I did before, even!"

Stupor leaned forward on the desk, propping his chin on crossed arms.

"Life here is weird compared to home," he continued. "Things get amplified a lot. The good things about life are a lot nicer here. I 'sorta' get accepted by some people here. I also get taken care of so I don't have to rely on getting money from employers that dislike me. The bad things about life are a lot worse, too. I found a new bully in the form of Mr. Lanzendorf.

"Hey, you know why I did that thing at the group therapy about Mr. Lanzendorf? I wanted some more self-validation that even if we actually did complain about him, we wouldn't be heard. I wanted to know for sure that they wouldn't even listen to us because we're crazy. I wanted to know it even though I knew it would just make me feel worse about being here. And sure enough, Dr. Goodrich didn't even seem to bat an eye.

"Hey, you know what? Just because of that, I

don't even feel like I'm as accepted as I thought I was anymore. Now it feels more like they tolerate us just because we're too innocent for jail, yet too guilty for freedom. Man, this asylum is like punishment limbo!"

"Ich hasse es, wenn du so viel redest, aber wenigstens sind deine Ideen faszinierend," Jörg mumbled, facing away from Stupor.

Stupor suddenly jolted his head up and looked to Jörg.

"Hey, do you happen to know where that huge muscle guy is from this morning?" he asked.

Jörg lazily twirled his hand in the air and mumbled, "Meine Quellen sagen mir, dass man ihn inzwischen schon weggeschickt haben sollte, aber wegen der Politik ist er noch immer hier."

"I... I don't really know what that means, but thanks, Jörg. I do hope I see him again. He really broke the monotony of this place."

Jörg gave a small chuckle in response. Stupor then turned off the light to the cell and climbed into his top bunk. He covered himself up and drifted to sleep as he admired the stars through the window's outer bars.

***

"I am a lovely butterfly...
I hate butterflies.
Oh, but how I love potatoes."

Chapter Three

Stupor woke up from a peaceful, dreamless sleep. He looked about the room, mildly groggy. Jörg was nowhere to be seen.

Speaking of Jörg, I can't remember the last time I've had a good bratwurst, he thought to himself as he dressed.

Putting on yet another identical orange shirt, he peered out his window, observing the inmates plodding about the courtyard. He noticed a few practicing basketball shots while some others—from what Stupor was able to infer—played Four Square, using their imaginations for the lines.

He stepped into the hall and noticed more patients gossiping with each other than usual.

Stupor decided to approach a lone woman not far from him, named Jade Morris. She was a particularly young patient at an even twenty years old. She was suffering from an advanced stage of anorexia, causing her face to look pale and sickly, dark circles tracing the undersides of her eyes. Her lanky figure only enhanced her appearance in an unflattering manner. She never bothered to fix her hair, causing it to hang down around her and frizz out like a blonde burlap sack.

"What's the word, milady?" Stupor asked her. "Something happen?"

She shied away from Stupor and eyed him with caution. After suspiciously checking around her, she opened her mouth to speak.

"Do you remember that big guy that hurt the

guards yesterday?" she asked sheepishly.

Stupor gasped. Excited, he ran away from her without bothering to continue the conversation. Realizing his folly, he returned.

"My apologies. Where is he?" Stupor asked, pitter-pattering his feet with rampant, unfettered enthusiasm. "He's still here, right?"

"He might be over in the commons... I don't really know," she responded, taking a few more steps back and avoiding eye contact.

Thanking her, Stupor bolted for the stairs of the building. He was reprimanded by a guard in passing, after which he slowed to the briskest walk he could muster.

Before long, he arrived at the commons with only one goal in mind: today, he was definitely going to make a friend.

Entering the building, he looked about and instantly noticed where patient C26 was located. Near one of the room's far corners, there was an area that was completely devoid of inmates. In its center sat patient C26, arms firmly crossed and face angrily scowling just as the day they met. Stupor approached him and waved his hand emphatically.

"Hey! Do you remember me?" Stupor asked with delight.

Recognizing him, C26 shot him a furious glare before returning his gaze to the room's corner. Stupor began to notice inmates watching him carefully. He placed his hands behind his back and turned back to C26.

"How did you get so strong?" he asked, trying his best to be friendly and personable.

C26 ignored him and kept his gaze forward. Stupor remained in place, undeterred.

"Why are you here?" he continued.

"Because of you miserable, honorless scum," he muttered in reply without breaking his stare.

Stupor fought the urge to dance in response to C26's voluntary communication. His hand twitched with pulse-pounding excitement.

"Yeah," he empathized. "That's why I'm here, too."

C26 quickly sneered at Stupor's contraction.

"Listening to you weaklings speak is the last thing I need right now. Leave me alone or else," he threatened.

"I'm not speaking correctly?"

C26 turned and stared at Stupor, irritated.

"I am warning you, boy. Go away."

Stupor sat for a moment, trying to think of anything else he could say. His thoughts were prematurely interrupted by Officer Abernathy, who had approached from behind.

"B256," he commanded. "You need to get away from C26."

Stupor turned around and stamped his foot in a huff, stating, "I was only talking to him!"

"That's the problem," the guard replied. "Get away now or I will restrain you."

Stupor glanced at C26 and saw that he had returned his attention to the wall. After glancing back at the guard, he walked to a nearby table and sat down with his head propped up on one hand. He chose to amuse himself by running the index finger of his other hand along the surface of the table in a circular motion.

Lanzendorf entered the common room just as Abernathy returned to his post next to the door. Lanzendorf stopped to look the guard up and down with a cynical look on his face.

"How is C26?" he asked him.

"He's doing fine, sir," Abernathy affirmed. "Patient B256 was found talking to him again. Borderline antagonizing. I made him cease and desist."

Lanzendorf raised an eyebrow, curious. He glanced over at Stupor and watched him as he argued with his hand, fashioned like a puppet.

"He was antagonizing him?" the tyrant asked rhetorically. "It's a shame you noticed the boy."

"Er... Is it, sir?"

"Well, I suppose in this case any outcome is a good one. A win-win situation, hm?" Lanzendorf mused as he walked away, a mischievous smile creeping across his face.

He extracted his cell phone and held it to his ear. Surreptitiously, he strode briskly past Stupor while pretending to speak to someone on it.

"I'm certainly glad to hear that C26 is more cooperative," he said to no one in particular. "In that case, I will decrease the security and reform them to their original posts. The sooner C26 can make friends, the sooner he can stop being such a barbarian toward staff."

C26, hearing him, loudly uttered, "Negative."

Stupor also overheard the conversation as per Lanzendorf's intent, and his resolve to befriend C26 had been reinvigorated. He glanced back at the guards posted near the main entrance and saw Lanzendorf giving them commands prior to a large number leaving. He looked around the room, formulating a plan to communicate with C26.

Getting up, Stupor moved to the board game area of the room and searched for a scrap of paper and pencil inside one of the boxes. Sure enough, he managed to find such a game and extracted the materials needed for writing a note.

Stupor moved back to his original table and quickly scribbled a short message on it. He then crumpled up the note and tossed it onto C26's table. C26 noticed the crushed ball of paper and casually tossed it over his shoulder and onto the floor.

Stupor then briefly glanced about the room and noticed several inmates watching him again. He sneakily picked up the paper and tossed it onto C26's desk again.

The now lone Officer Abernathy moved to interrupt Stupor, but was stopped by Lanzendorf.

"Let him go," he ordered, smiling devilishly at Stupor.

"Sir... seriously?"

"Sometimes to maintain order, people need a little taste of chaos. This helps them appreciate the control they are under. This boy didn't learn from his last encounter with C26, so I propose that this time we allow him to learn."

"Understood, sir." Abernathy acknowledged, impressed. "B256 can't learn his place from us, so we'll let him learn it himself."

Lanzendorf merely smirked and watched the unfolding situation.

C26 picked up the paper and looked around to see Stupor nearby, giving him a thumbs up. Grumpily, he unfolded the note and read it.

Dear Big Ol' Guy,

I'm very interested in why you're here, even if you think I won't believe you. What's the problem with my talking? How come you hate contractions so much? Do you also hate them if I write them?

From Your New Friend,
Baron Von Stupor

C26 furiously smashed the paper back into a little ball and stood up. "Damned contractions!" he shouted. "Stop using them!"

With all of his might, C26 threw the ball at Stupor only to watch it bounce harmlessly off of his mask.

"I'm sorry," he apologized, totally unfazed by the paper ball. "I really don't mean to. I guess it's just a force of habit. For a friend, though, I'm more than willing to try my best!"

C26 clenched his head and roared prior to lunging at Stupor. He wriggled awkwardly out of his arms, but was then grabbed by the neck and yanked close.

"I have lost my patience with you, Terran!" C26 shouted at Stupor's face. "I hereby challenge you to Honorable Resolution! If I win, you are to leave me alone forever!"

Finishing his statement, C26 pushed Stupor away. Stupor failed to maintain balance and fell down from the tremendous force.

The patients were all quiet and too scared to come to Stupor's aid.

What the hell is Honorable Resolution? thought Lanzendorf to himself as he watched the tense situation unfold.

"Honorable Resolution? Is that some kind of game or something?" Stupor asked the scowling giant while rubbing his neck.

"Strictly defined, yes," he answered. "It is a game played only by true warriors of my clan and foolish Terrans that think they stand any chance against us. It is a game of pride and honor, and the only way of understanding who is superior to whom! Now, Baron Von Stupor, you may choose where we will compete!"

"Well hang on there, big buddy! We all know what happens if you win, but what about if I win?"

"Pah. If you, a wretched, pathetic, infantile, derelict, insignificant Terran, can even walk away from our battle with your life intact I will happily forgive any and all contraction usage of yours."

"Sounds like a steal! Does that mean that we can also be friends?"

"No. I will despise you until my dying breath and will relish the thought of your blood on my hands."

"You've got some creepy metaphors, man."

On hearing Stupor's next contraction, C26 cringed and demanded, "Enough of this banter! Choose the location so that we may settle our wager!"

"Is this an inside game or an outside game?"

"I do not care! Hurry up and choose so that I may smash you into the dirt and return to my silent complaining!"

"You know, silent complaining never solves anything."

C26 gritted his teeth and glared at Stupor so hard his eyes were practically popping out of his head.

"Sheesh!" Stupor exclaimed. "You're a poor sport before the game even begins! I suppose that just in case this game requires a lot of movement, we should play outside. Maybe the basketball court is available!"

C26 immediately began walking toward the common room entrance. Stupor briskly followed, happy and excited.

I'm finally going to play a game with someone! he thought to himself with a bounce in his step. *A real non-checkers game with a real person who is mostly sane instead of only partially sane!*

The patients followed the two outside, hardly sure of what to do. Every one of them recognized C26's dangerous potential, and it seemed like that very potential was stopping everyone from preventing an impending massacre.

In the meantime, Lanzendorf had assembled his entire security staff in the CCTV room. After clicking the mouse a few times, a full-screen feed of Stupor and patient C26 on the basketball court popped into view.

"I want you all to see this!" he called out to his staff. "Especially you, Ralph." he mentioned to the blank-faced boy sitting right next to him.

"Yup," he uttered.

"Mr. 'Baron Von Stupor' here is soon going to feel a lot of pain. I want him to feel it and I want you all to see him feeling it. I want you all to remember that this is what happens to those who cross me.

"I have ultimate power in this facility. I see all and I know all. I have direct influence over the decisions that the board of directors makes. Even if any of you decide to part ways with this establishment and work elsewhere, your future career anywhere depends on me.

"Patient B256 is going to be an example of what I can do to people. It can happen to these crazies, it can happen to guards, it can happen to anyone who even thinks of defying the empire I have created here. In this place I am Alpha and Omega, gentlemen. I am the beginning and the end.

"Now sit and watch this kid get everything that's been coming to him."

"Yup," Ralph uttered once more.

A circle was formed around the basketball court, with C26 and Stupor standing directly in the center.

"Lookit that!" Stupor glowed. "Seems like we have spectators, er... I don't really know what to call you. What's your name?"

C26 simply snarled at Stupor.

"Do you not have a name or something? You seem awfully grumpy about it. You know what? You seem like a real 'Baron Von Poorly Spelled Vengence' kind of guy."

"Are you ready to begin?!" C26 roared.

"Now hang on just one second, Vengence!" Stupor responded, tapping his chin in thought. "Yeah! Man, Vengence rolls right off the tongue! What a cool name! I'll just call you Vengence for short and we can be some sort of Team Baron! The Baron Brothers! Comrades a la Barron!"

Glowering in disgust, C26 declared, "Ready or not, it is time for you to die!"

The inmates were frozen with fear as C26 thundered toward Stupor with amazing speed despite his size.

Stupor, noticing he had been very distracted, turned toward C26 and began to ask a question. He then realized fast action was necessary as a running haymaker was flying straight toward his face. Based on its speed and proximity, Stupor judged that it clearly was not intended to miss.

Chapter Four

Noticing C26's fist flying directly toward his face, Stupor quickly used his arm to swat at it. Though he was clearly too weak to bat it away, he at least managed to propel himself out of its path and into an awkward pirouette.

Spinning once, he came to a stop while C26 briefly stumbled over his own feet. Stupor then wheeled back around and placed an open palm on C26's right shoulder blade.

"Tag! You're 'IT', buddy!" Stupor gloated as C26 froze, incredulous.

C26 turned and blinked at Stupor in morbid confusion. The inmates found themselves just as confounded.

"We're playing Tag, correct?" Stupor asked, oblivious. "Or at least that's what I thought we were playing."

Regaining his resolve, C26 put on a heavy frown and lunged once more, attempting a heavy right uppercut. Stupor, rather than being hit by it, grabbed onto C26's monstrous fist and used its force to give him a boost backwards and into the air. Stupor's head reached to just above C26's before he fell back down, stumbling over his feet and tumbling backward. He performed a backward roll and somersaulted right back to his feet.

C26 impatiently charged forth at Stupor with everything he had, throwing a dizzying flurry of jabs. Remaining stalwart against the frightening wall of fists, Stupor nimbly shifted his weight and pushed C26's wrists away to redirect the blows in off directions. Noticing the ineffectiveness of his rush, C26 took a step back and attempted a left high kick toward Stupor's head. Detecting this, Stupor nimbly cartwheeled to the side, out of its range. The kick was a complete miss and C26's back became exposed once again.

The giant turned around, but by then Stupor had gotten unexpectedly close and shouted in his face. C26 yelped in surprise and staggered back a few steps as Stupor stamped his foot and did a few silly poses.

The few patients that weren't agape began to clap. Tasting such appreciation, Stupor began to bounce eagerly, waving to random people.

"Hey Vengence," Stupor called with a happy chuckle. "You think they know we're just playing around?"

C26 was completely baffled. He lowered his guard and examined Stupor for a few moments.

"Are you... truly like the rest of them?" he asked in utter disbelief. "No Terran could evade my attacks with that kind of dexterity! What kind of discipline is your fighting? I demand to know!"

Stupor turned to face Vengence and jabbed his finger into the air. "Big bad bully bashing!" he answered prior to pumping his fist.

After Stupor's reply, C26's interest faded as he approached him with a straight kick. Stupor jumped high, straddling his leg. As C26 retracted his foot, Stupor landed flat on both feet, facing sideways with his left shoulder facing C26.

C26 motioned to throw a right hook and Stupor bobbed forward to duck under it. The hook was a feint, and C26 snatched Stupor by his neck with his left hand. He then held Stupor up and squeezed for a moment, watching him wriggle helplessly. The pressure against Stupor's throat elicited a morbid gurgle as he batted at Vengence's arm. As Stupor began to fade, C26 reared back his right fist and punched Stupor in his mask so hard he reciprocated, flipping a full 270 degrees and flopping helplessly into a prone position. Stupor lay motionless like a ragdoll.

The inmates appeared horrified at the sight and began to grow panicked, talking among each other and pointing at C26 in fear. A couple ran away toward a covered walkway leading into the security building.

Meanwhile, Lanzendorf propped himself up against the wall, laughing hysterically at the CCTV screen.

"Yes! Oh, yes!" he cried, tears running down his face. "Did you see him flip? Did you hear that smack? Oh my goodness!"

"That kid was dodging very well, though. I never knew he could move like that," Officer Herald commented.

"It's not about skill, my friend, it is about results. And these? These results are better than I could have imagined!"

"He... he could seriously kick someone's ass if he really wanted to," Herald continued, his mind completely blown.

C26 stood over Stupor's crumpled body and looked upon it as he cracked his knuckles.

"To my complete and utter surprise, Terran, you are a guileful opponent," C26 complimented him. "It is a shame that you were so ignorant and naïve, as you would have made a very fine slave." He then turned to the inmates and announced, "Let this be a lesson to anyone brave enough to confront me in..."

C26 stopped in mid-sentence once he heard sounds of movement coming from behind him. He wheeled around and was shocked to see the ragdoll standing up and coughing.

Stupor shook himself off and stood up very aggressively, his knees slightly bent and his fists tightly clenched.

"You weren't playing at all!" he accused C26, jabbing his finger angrily. "You were just trying to beat me up the whole time! What kind of manners do you have, to do that to a guy that just wants to be your friend? Don't be a meanass, Vengence!"

"What?!" cried Lanzendorf, agape. "He was knocked out! How in the world is he standing?!"

"I landed a hard punch in the center of your mask!" C26 exclaimed, baffled. "How is it not damaged? How are you still conscious?"

Suddenly, Stupor seemed to forget everything he was angry about. "Oh, this old thing?" he asked, rapping his mask. "Idunno how it works, but you can hit me in the face with a lead pipe and I wouldn't feel a thing through it."

"Is it wood?" he asked, approaching Stupor.

C26 grabbed the mask by one of its horns and tried to tug it. Like it were glued, Stupor was helplessly pulled with it and fell off his feet. He flailed angrily while C26 stared at him in utter disbelief. He gave it a slight shake and Stupor's body wobbled right along with it.

"Can it not be removed?" C26 wondered out loud.

Regaining his footing, Stupor wrenched his mask out of Vengence's firm grasp and spitefully slapped his hand away.

"Don't touch my mask! This thing's private!" he scolded, shying away and shielding it with his hands. "Whatever happened to manners, man?"

C26 gave Stupor a grumpy look and resumed his fighting stance. "I no longer care about your mask. This time I will break it," he threatened.

"I'm not fighting you! You're big and grumpy and violent and mean, but I know in my heart of hearts that deep down you're a really nice guy!"

"Stop using those damned contractions and fight me, you sniveling toddler!"

C26 dashed forward and tried to grab Stupor again, but Stupor was quick to the draw and clutched his arm. Stupor twirled himself around C26, winding up behind him. C26 kept his arm out and whirled around ferociously, attempting a backhanded blow. Stupor quickly rolled around and positioned himself behind C26 yet again.

"Come on, Vengence!" he pleaded. "Hey, if I

promise to stop using contractions forever, will you promise to stop trying to break my face off?"

"Stop calling me that, you imbecile! My name is not Vengence!" C26 roared while throwing a backward mule kick.

Stupor bobbed far to the left, the kick barely grazing him. C26 then swung his left arm wildly, causing Stupor to bob to the right.

C26 spun back around and the two found themselves facing each other.

"Well it's not like you'll bother to tell me your name! What else am I supposed to call you? C26 is not a name!" Stupor asked, making no attempt to fight as he stared straight into the furious eyes of his aggressor.

C26 tried a headbutt, but Stupor leaned back and out of the way. C26 next tried to perform a vicious hook aimed at the side of Stupor's head. To this, Stupor leaned farther back and limboed backward, his arms wiggling in the air to either side with each shuffle.

C26 trod forward to punt Stupor between his legs, but Stupor was quick to engage a lightning fast backflip. He awkwardly landed on his feet, doubled over. C26 continued his rush without slowing and reared his fist to throw an uppercut at him. Stupor looked up at him, helpless to react from such an awkward position.

"You never play checker Beeboo, assholio!" a familiar voice shouted, distracting both Stupor and C26.

Beeboo ran and struck C26 in the back with

his open hand. The impact of the feeble hand against the goliath was a barely audible, pitiful thwap. C26 turned to stare at him, morbidly offended.

"Beeboo know you really want play checker," insisted the manic patient, jabbing his finger at C26. "You not play checker and just stare at wall and make Beeboo mad! You learn good lesson now? You gonna play checker Beeboo?"

C26 gave Beeboo a horrified, offended stare while the patient leered back with his hands on his hips. Regaining himself, C26's face twisted to one of utter rage.

"How dare you interfere with an Honorable Resolution, you despicable Terran scum?!" C26 bellowed as he grabbed Beeboo by his arm and waist and hoisted him up above his head. Beeboo was immediately frightened and began to wail unintelligibly. "You must never interfere with an Honorable Resolution!"

C26 hurled Beeboo quite a distance, bowling over several other inmates in the process. This action caused many inmates to break their fear and rush C26 in anger while others ran away, screaming.

"Worthless creatures! I will defeat you all!" C26 declared, charging headlong into the crowd. He knocked out several inmates with crushing blows, but the sheer number of people proved to be overwhelming for him as he was swiftly buried underneath the raging mob. The last thing he remembered seeing to his complete dismay, was

Stupor loyally defending him. Trying his absolute best, Stupor pulled inmates off of him; any that were hostile toward him he nonviolently evaded and pushed out of the way.

"Sir," Abernathy spoke. "Inmates are getting hurt out there. I really think we should go break up the riot."

Lanzendorf waved his hand dismissively, but his eyes remained furiously locked on the screen. His smile long gone, he watched the chaos and festered in a silent rage.

Well done, B256, he thought. *Once the board hears of this it will be by far the worst humiliation I will have ever experienced by your hands. You will pay dearly for it.*

Chapter Five

"How dare you started a riot in my asylum?" Lanzendorf sternly asked Stupor inside his office.

"I'd like to think of it as starting itself," Stupor rebutted, lazily slouching in his chair.

"Oh? I have security footage here of you fighting the inmates with your gigantic friend."

"I've been getting the feeling lately that he doesn't like me very much."

"B256, I don't think you understand your predicament here. This nonsense is all I need to get you put on a stricter program. I hope you enjoy isolation, since you'll be experiencing a lot more of it very soon."

"What is Vengence's real name? I'm starting to think it rhymes with a bad word or something, because he really doesn't want to share it. Is it Chuck?"

Lanzendorf, his temper flipping like a switch, banged both of his fists on his desk with all of his might.

"Doesn't anything bother you?!" he shouted. "What is it with that empty skull of yours that you can't pay attention to reality for a fraction of a second?! You have no future here! None! I will personally make sure of that!"

Sitting up, Stupor asked, "Hey, how long do I have to stay here? I have to use the bathroom, plus I already know this lecture. We've only had this exchange a bajillion times already."

Lanzendorf felt his face begin boil with anger

but quickly regained himself, hiding behind his smug grin. He leaned in his chair and interlaced his fingers as Stupor bobbed back and forth in his seat.

"Here's what we're going to do," Lanzendorf began. "I fear not only for your safety, but also that of your fellow inmates. Therefore, I will be revoking your privilege to wear street clothes.

"In addition to this, you will be confined to an isolation chamber indefinitely, for purposes of investigation. Pending the board's approval, you will then be allowed to roam freely among your peers once more.

"Now, get out of my damn office and report to Officer Herald waiting outside. He will escort you to an examination room for new check-ins where you can change into some medical scrubs, which will be your new wardrobe for the rest of your life. Enjoy."

Lanzendorf then turned to his computer, ignoring Stupor, and moved his hands to type. Looking down at his keyboard, his grin slowly faded. He noticed that several keys were now broken off and the frame cracked from when he slammed his fists on his desk.

He immediately jumped out of his chair and stomped behind his desk in anger. "*Goddamn it, you did it again!*" he exploded with hatred. "*I hate you so much! Get out of my office!*"

Stupor got out of his chair and ran out of the room laughing as Lanzendorf threw his various office supplies at him.

Stupor ducked around the corner on exiting, just narrowly dodging a stapler. Officer Herald looked at him, completely surprised.

"What did you do?" he asked Stupor, stifling a chuckle himself.

"Oh, more like he does it to himself," Stupor replied, his hands on his knees.

Herald did not reply as the two began to walk down the hall toward patient check-in. They approached what appeared to be a dark hole in the wall, and Stupor could hear someone talking inside. Suddenly, C26's voice was very loudly heard.

"You are the only person I have ever met that is worse than a Terran," he said without remorse. "If it were not for your drunken swaying, I would suspect you to be catatonic!"

Stupor stuck his head inside and saw C26 sitting with Ralph. The hole itself almost seemed carved out, lit only by Ralph's decrepit computer monitor. Part of the desk had an unidentifiable slime on it and his trash bin was overflowing with snack wrappers. C26 sat inside, severely hunched and barely able to fit. He appeared just as sour as ever.

Is this really Ralph's office? Stupor wondered to himself. *It seems smaller than an isolation chamber.*

"I need your information, sir. It's an incident report," Ralph wheezed to C26, barely noticing Stupor's intrusion. "Box number one... name."

"Let's go, B256," Herald nagged.

"But wait! I think I can help!" Stupor replied.

"He mentioned his name?" Herald asked, his curiosity piqued.

"No, but I bet a hundred dollars I know what it is! I figured it out in my head!"

Herald seemed skeptical, but waved his hand permissively.

"Make it quick," he warned.

"Box number one... name," Ralph mumbled, staring at his tiny computer screen. "I was told to fill this box and all of the other boxes in... Mr. Lanzendorf wants it."

"Ask me all you want for my information and I will firmly repeat myself every time. You are an unintelligent slug that bridges the line between sentience and lifelessness," C26 spat in response.

"Hey Ralph! I'd be willing to bet his name is Baron Von Poorly Spelled Vengence!" Stupor suggested.

"That's enough, B256. I never should have let you in there," Herald said, pulling lightly on Stupor's arm.

"Negative," C26 responded sharply, glaring at Stupor. "Call me John Doe. I am not Vengence."

"Okay," Ralph agreed.

"No wait! That's not a good name for you, Vengence!" Stupor persisted as he was ushered away.

"I am not Vengence!" C26 insisted as Stupor left around the corner.

"Don't forget, Ralph!" Stupor shouted, by now barely audible. "No A because it's poorly spelled! And capitalize every V!"

"Okay," Ralph agreed.

"You had better not name me Vengence, boy!" C26 threatened. "I am John Doe!"

"Okay."

Ralph slowly typed in the name 'John Doe', but the program returned an error.

"John Doe is already in use here, sir. I need another name," he said apathetically.

Ralph then deleted 'John Doe' from the box, slowly depressing the 'backspace' key with each letter. C26 crossed his arms angrily and said nothing.

"If you don't give me your name, I'm gonna have to go with that other name that the guy in the mask said. It's all I got."

C26 glared down the hall Stupor went and back at Ralph's unfazed stare. He then sneered and leaned against the wall, defeated.

Growing confused, Ralph began typing the report, occasionally pausing to see if C26—who was now officially known as Baron Von Poorly Spelled Vengence—would object.

"Why do you always have to cause trouble?" Herald asked Stupor, handing him some medical scrubs. "It's like you're driven to be the center of attention."

"Well, good sir, I ask you this:" Stupor asked back. "What would anyone do when they can't catch a break no matter how hard they try? They can't get what they want, so they make the most of what they've got and try to make things as fun as possible!"

"Well, what do you want?"

"Right now? A bratwurst, actually. I've been craving them lately."

"Get dressed," Herald flatly instructed with a sigh, closing the examination room door and waiting outside.

After dressing himself, Stupor was escorted back past Ralph and the patient now known as Baron Von Poorly Spelled Vengence.

"Why do you insist my name be something as senseless as Vengence?!" he asked Stupor angrily.

Without stopping, Stupor replied, "I figured you didn't care what you were called, since you don't seem to want to tell anybody what your real name is!"

"It is a stupid name!"

"I'm sure your real name isn't stupid, buddy! Have some pride in yourself!"

"T-that is not what I... argh!"

Vengence squeezed his fists in irritation as Stupor was by then too far away to talk to.

Stupor and Officer Herald stopped in front of an isolation chamber. Herald opened the door and ushered Stupor inside.

"So what about my appointments?" he asked the guard.

"We'll escort you to them and then escort you back to this cell." Herald responded without looking at him.

"When can I come out?"

"I don't know. You're going to be in there for a while this time, though. What you did was serious and if you don't get a board approval, you'll probably stay in there indefinitely or be shipped off to a higher security facility."

Officer Herald shut the chamber door and walked away. Stupor stood in place for a few moments and then lay down on his bed.

I do get needlessly blamed for a lot of stuff, but I think I am sorta at fault for this one, he thought to himself. *However, Vengence is certainly a lot more communicative toward me! That's probably the only plus to this situation.*

The biggest problem is that now Mr. Lanzendorf took away my clothes! Those were the last things that really kept me individualized here. Now I'm just a number. I'm just a stupid number with a stupid mask.

***

"They don't deserve the freedom they are blessed with, don't you think? They do all of this to me; imagine what they do to others who are different, too. People are human, and humans are impressionable. They can be guided toward reason. They should be punished. Who are we to punish them? Do people deserve punishment for being different? For thinking differently? The greatest acts of kindness are those performed by complete strangers. Punishment! I like to see the good in all people. Kindness begets kindness! Kindness begets betrayal! Bratwurst..."

***

"Hello," greeted Dr. Erika Pedilla-Perez as she entered the board meeting room with a stressed look on her face. "Exciting day, huh?"

"You can sure say that again," Dr. Goodrich replied, glancing at the nearby wall clock. "Now we're just waiting on Sean."

The meeting room was ornate, with beautiful paintings on the deep green painted walls. The five directors' chairs sat on the back end of a wide table near the end of the room.

Dr. Perez barely glanced at Lanzendorf as she passed, sitting in her chair and extracting a small pad of paper from her handbag.

Not long after, a stocky Sean Ritzo entered the room, cleaning a pair of eyeglasses with his shirt. He marched briskly past Lanzendorf and to his seat beside the other directors.

"Sorry everyone, I was right in the middle of rolling out new software," he explained with his usual nasal shrill. He then looked at Lanzendorf and jabbed his finger. "And Mr. Lanzendorf, I keep telling you that I can't fix a laptop when all you write on the ticket is that it's broken. Where it says 'describe the problem' you're supposed to actually describe what is the problem."

"The problem is that it's broken," he replied with a faint sneer. "Do you really need to be told how to do your job from there?"

Sean opened his mouth to argue, but was cut short by Mr. Bark.

"Mr. Lanzendorf, we have a particularly huge problem here," Mr. Bark said to him inside of the board of directors' meeting room.

"I just don't understand how this mess could have happened during my absence," Lanzendorf responded, primly standing with his hands over his belt buckle.

"You were gone?" Mr. Bark asked, surprised. "Where did you go?"

"I was recovering from a nasty stomach bug today, possibly onset by the country fried steak I ate yesterday. I spent some time in the restroom, and asked Officer Abernathy to monitor things while I was in the restroom."

"Mr. Lanzendorf, I'm sure you're well aware of how employee performance reflects strongly on management," Dr. Goodrich mentioned to him. "He should have known how to react to this situation. How could it have escalated so far without any employee interference?"

"I believe Officer Abernathy to be a bit more green to catastrophes than he led me to believe. I should have seen this in him with my intuition, and I accept full responsibility for his actions."

"Now hold on," Mr. Jenkins interjected. "If you were sick and Abernathy screwed up, then he does deserve some if not all of the heat for this. You definitely should have had a better grip on him, but for the time this whole debacle was going down that issue would be on Abernathy's hands."

"I'd like to add something," mentioned Dr. Perez. "Despite the brutality we saw in the video, none of the inmates were badly hurt. Plenty are sore, but only patient B262 is staying for further examination. This could have been a lot worse."

"I suppose that unless anyone has something to add, we can dismiss Mr. Lanzendorf?" Mr. Bark suggested.

After a few moments had passed, Lanzendorf was dismissed and Stupor was brought into the room.

"I am very shocked with these recent events," Mr. Bark said to him with furrowed brows. "Of all people, I have the hardest time believing that you would be capable of creating an air of such violence. However, because of my faith in you, I want to hear your side of the story."

"I'm not so willing to listen," Dr. Goodrich added. "But I'd be kidding if I said I wasn't the slightest bit curious what you have to say for yourself."

"Well, thank you for having me," Stupor said with a light bow. "I've always wondered what the admin area looks like!"

"Tell us what happened out there, Stupor," Mr. Jenkins instructed Stupor coldly.

"Well, I didn't cause any ruckus," he quickly affirmed. "If you look on the cameras, you'll see we were playing Tag."

"What about the part where you were hit so hard that you did that backflip before landing on your face?" Dr. Goodrich interrogated. "Is that when you were 'IT'?"

"Oh man! Can you see that well? I'd like to watch it sometime. Can I have a copy?"

The directors eyed him suspiciously. Seeing this, Stupor straightened himself back up and focused.

"Oh yeah! And about that," he rambled. "I think we've confirmed that Vengence is super big and super strong, right? Well, turns out he's also super clumsy. It was a total accident!"

"There were punches and kicks involved! Do you really expect me to believe you were playing Tag with this man?" Dr. Goodrich debated.

"Well, it turns out we both practiced martial arts at a time in our lives. So the Tag you see here isn't the Tag you know. It's sort of a game and training exercise hybrid! I can show you what I mean, if you like! It can be done by people of all skill and experience levels, and it teaches you a lot about yourself!"

"Stupor, I would like you to give one reason why I should believe any word you say over this video that clearly shows you being punched in your face."

"Well, I'm best friends with Vengence and he talks to me. As far as I know, that's a lot more than you've been able to accomplish, sir."

The directors looked at Dr. Goodrich, who now bore an angry scowl. "I don't believe you," he said, insulted by Stupor's challenging remark. "Prove it to me right here."

"I walked past Vengence on the way here; I'm guessing you're gonna try to talk to him, right?" Stupor inquired. "Let me pass him on the way out. He'll talk to me, and if he says anything to you guys it'll probably just be some anti-earthling hate speech. I bet you!"

"I move to grant his request," Dr. Goodrich challenged.

"I second," Mr. Bark agreed. "All in favor?"

Without hesitation, the five directors raised their hands in favor of Stupor's request. He gave his arm a happy swing and turned to walk away.

"On a last note," Stupor added, glancing at them from over his shoulder. "I'd like you guys to remember that Bebop interrupted the whole thing by smacking Vengence, and Vengence has known temper issues when antagonized."

"We'll remember," Mr. Bark affirmed. "Go ahead and leave and you may do your test on the way out."

The guards escorted Vengence in, who shot Stupor a grumpy look.

"Hey there, friend! That warm-up outside was more fun than expected, huh?" he asked with a chuckle.

Vengence thought to himself for a moment and grumbled, "Yes, and a bit enlightening."

The other directors were impressed while Dr. Goodrich continued to frown heavily at Stupor. Ignoring the doctor, he waddled out the door, uttering "blub, blub, blub".

"Patient C26, or... Baron Von Poorly Spelled Vengence, we'd like to know your side of what happened outside," Mr. Bark said to Vengence.

"Your baldness is a sign of your impending weakness, old man," Vengence growled, crossing his arms. "You Terrans age poorly."

Mr. Bark furrowed his brows at Vengence and waved his hand dismissively. Vengence was then escorted out of the room.

"Wow, Stupor called it right on the mark," observed Mr. Ritzo.

"I still think he's simply a manipulator and an ingenious liar," Dr. Goodrich shot back.

"Regardless, we need to handle this situation with utmost care or it could get ugly," Mr. Bark warned them. "There are three solid facts here: The security guards were not present when they should have been, the incident reports–prepared by Mr. Lanzendorf's new hire, I might add–are utterly useless, and Beeboo was the catalyst that caused the actual riot itself."

"Hang on," Mr. Jenkins cut in. "C26 threw the man at other inmates."

"Did he attack the patients, or did he simply throw Beeboo who landed on the patients?" Mr. Bark retorted. "Also, as Stupor did mention, if Beeboo had never interrupted whatever those two were doing, the patients would not have grown violent toward C26."

The other directors were quiet. Dr. Goodrich remained sulking in his seat.

"I move to give Stupor benefit of the doubt and allow him to roam freely among the other patients," Mr. Bark announced. "However, I feel he should still have his street clothing privileges revoked because regardless of everything else, he was still engaged in dangerous activities."

"I second that," Sean agreed.

"All in favor?" Mr. Bark asked as he, Mr. Ritzo, and Dr. Perez all raised their hands. "The motion for Stupor to cease isolation and have his clothing privileges revoked is passed."

"I move that Officer Abernathy be demoted from his Lead Officer position and an opening be made for said position," Dr. Perez announced. "I'd also like to add to this movement that due to the severity of the incident, Officer Abernathy be placed on final notice."

"I second that," Dr. Goodrich agreed.

"All in favor?" Mr. Bark asked as everyone but Mr. Jenkins raised their hands. "The motion to demote Officer Abernathy is passed. I would like to wait until tomorrow to put this particular motion in effect, therefore tomorrow will be Mr. Abernathy's last day as the Lead Officer. Is there anything else to address or shall we adjourn?"

The directors all remained silent and the meeting was concluded.

Chapter Six

Stupor was startled awake by people arguing outside the isolation chamber door. As he slowly regained awareness, he recognized the voices as Lanzendorf and Officer Herald.

"Do not let him out!" Lanzendorf demanded furiously.

"Sir, you don't understand! The decision was made by the board of directors. I have to let him go," he defended, opening the door. "Come out, patient B256."

Stupor stepped out of the cell and stood right between the two men. "Howdy, y'all!" he greeted happily.

Lanzendorf grabbed the smiling patient by his shoulders and roughly shoved him toward the exit at the end of the hall. Stupor stumbled for a moment before catching himself. He did a silly dance directed at Lanzendorf, stamping his feet and swinging his arms before leaving through the door.

"Enjoy your freedom, you little imp! It won't last much longer!" Lanzendorf shouted after him. He then leered at Herald. "The board voted this, did they? We'll just see how long that decision lasts."

Lanzendorf then stormed off into his office, sharply ordering Ralph to get him some coffee. As he stepped behind his desk, Abernathy came storming in after him.

"I got demoted?!" he cried in anger.

"Apparently. It was news to me when I came in this morning," Lanzendorf responded while sitting down in his chair.

"My mom's gonna kill me! Why the hell am I demoted?!"

"My first guess is politics. Looking at the facts, we're taking heat for yesterday and B256 is still roaming free with the other inmates against my strict orders. The board is sympathizing with C26 because they believe he is so embittered that he cannot function properly.

"My personal belief is that B256 managed to finagle the board into seeing himself and C26 as the victims while security takes the full blame for not being present."

Abernathy gave Lanzendorf a skeptical scowl and jabbed his finger angrily.

"Security wasn't there because you made us watch some stupid fight on the cameras because of your dumb grudge against B256!" he accused. "This whole thing is your fault, sir!"

"Mine?!"

"This wouldn't have happened if you had just let me do my job in the common room!"

Lanzendorf slapped his desk with both hands and rose in his chair, meeting Abernathy's gaze.

"I made you what you are today, boy!" he shouted. "Don't get sucked into the steaming pile of political crap the directors are trying to drop on the security department! Don't you see what's going on here?!"

"No sir, I don't! I'd love to know!"

"That idiot is what's going on!" Lanzendorf insisted, pointing out the bay window.

"Oh, Christ," Abernathy sighed.

"Listen to me, Abernathy! I hate that kid, but he definitely hates us too. He's more intelligent than he leads us to believe, right?"

"Yeah."

"And he has many issues with obeying figures of authority, right?"

"Yeah?"

"And he has been pulling antics ever since he first arrived here, right?"

"What's your point?"

Lanzendorf pointed out the bay window once again while maintaining his authoritative stare at Abernathy.

"C26 is the actual catalyst here," he said with confidence. "B256 wants to bring us down, more specifically me. That's why he wants to be friends with C26 so badly. He's working that man like a pawn just like he's working anyone else he can. His manipulation is infecting my empire and trying to turn everyone else against me.

"He is a blight on this facility. Everything was fine until he got here. I've had him mostly under control, but once C26 arrived the chips began to fall in his favor."

Abernathy stood in deep thought.

"I pulled for you at the board meeting, but B256 went before me," Lanzendorf continued. "Whatever he said at that meeting, it was meant to eliminate my number two from the equation.

That number two is you, and even though you're no longer the lead officer after today, you're still number two to me. I managed to retain your job, so you should be thanking me."

"You're really egomaniacal, you know that?" Abernathy said to him, hands on his hips. "...but I think you're right about B256 and C26. If we get rid of them, everything will be good again?"

"Things will definitely be under control if we can get rid of C26. C26 is B256's trump card. After that, B256 is mine."

Abernathy nodded and said, "Tell me what I need to do."

***

Stupor strolled into the common room and grabbed one of the last trays of food. Not seeing Vengence anywhere, he sat down at a random table and began to eat.

He pulled up his mask ever slightly, requiring a bit of brute strength from one of his hands to hold it up. Despite the mask's strange resistance to being moved about his face, he had developed a few decent strategies for feeding himself. The process still remained a headache for Stupor, but a headache he has since grown to tolerate.

He abruptly looked off to the side, letting his mask return to a neutral position. Sitting nearby was Beeboo, watching him with nervous eyes. They looked at each other for a few moments before Beeboo scooted further away.

"No, no... No play checker with Beeboo no more," he said, looking mildly worried.

Stupor glanced about the room and realized the inmates now seemed to be watching him and gossiping. They seemed to stray away from him, much like they treated Vengence. Hardly fazed, he returned to his eating.

Unable to see anything, he yelped when he felt a strong thud on the table. His mask snapped back into its place and he saw Vengence sitting across from him on the opposing bench.

"You are a very strange man," Vengence said to him with a curious expression on his face.

"Oh?" he replied in surprise.

"All I have done since we met is chastise and belittle you in front of everyone, and yet you still helped me outside. Why did you do it?"

"You're the only guy here who doesn't have friends of any kind, Vengence."

"I do not want Terran stravag as friends. But for Terran stravag, I suppose you are not so bad... in your own special way."

Stupor immediately shot straight up in his seat, pulsing with excitement. "Does that mean we're actually friends?" he energetically asked.

"I told you just a moment ago that I do not want friends! Do not expect me to associate with you! I acknowledge your existence. Be thankful I grant you that much; it is far more credit than I have ever given anyone else since I arrived here. And stop using those contractions!"

Stupor nodded and the two sat in silence.

Vengence observed the security guards near the main entrance.

"So what exactly would I have to do for us to be friends?" Stupor asked.

"We are not friends, now stop annoying me!" Vengence answered sharply.

Another brief moment of silence passed as Vengence surveyed the commons. He propped his head on his hand and looked at the security guards. One of them appeared to be ill rested and lazily looked about.

"I will escape this damned place if it is the last thing I ever do," he commented.

"You know, you seem just like the kind of guy to do that!" Stupor responded merrily.

Vengence gave him a grumpy look and asked, "What is that supposed to mean?"

"Well, you're a pretty huge guy, right? If it weren't for the tranquilizer and stun batons, I'm sure you could bowl anybody over!"

"I will not sit here if you continue to attack me with those contractions!"

"Wait a minute. Didn't you say before that you'd forgive my contraction usage if I survived our game yesterday?"

Vengence raised his eyebrows, surprised by Stupor's sudden remark. "I... I suppose I did," he awkwardly uttered in reply.

"Are you gonna do it?" Stupor asked with a smile.

Vengence looked very uncomfortable as he balled up his fist. He sat in total silence, thinking deeply. "Our wager was legitmate. I am bound by my honor, however unfortunate, to respect it," he resigned through gritted teeth. "Our battle saw no victor, but you did survive it."

"Thanks, buddy! I promise not to abuse it or rub it in your face or anything."

Stupor gave Vengence a friendly thumbs up, though he didn't appear to notice. He continued watching the security guards with a grumpy gaze, ultimately resting his head on top of crossed arms.

"Those cowards hide behind their weapons because they fear me in unarmed combat," he commented.

"I thought it was more to protect life and property?" Stupor asked. "You know, the whole security guard credo?"

"Hmph. Terrans and their worthless ideals. Locking me in here like some caged animal is a disgrace to their honor and my own!"

"Well, I tell you what. Since we're friends and all, I—"

"We are not friends!" Vengence snapped at him nastily.

"Oh," Stupor acknowledged without missing a beat. "I guess if we're not friends, I'll give this to someone else, then." Stupor then leaned back and surreptitiously extracted a thin object from his pants' waistband. He then slid it underneath Vengence's crossed arms.

Vengence's face twisted in raw agitation as he lifted his arms, revealing a key card. His sourness completely faded as he recognized it. He looked up at Stupor, who was vigorously nodding his head.

"When and how did you get this?" he asked, thoroughly suspicious.

"I took it from a guard," he said discretely. "Like I said, you seem just like the kind of guy who would try to escape. Therefore, I want to help you!"

Vengence looked down at the card and then back at Stupor, debating in his head. He then picked up the card and held it discretely in his hand while giving Stupor a very suspicious look.

"When you free yourself," Stupor murmured, leaning closer. "go visit a restaurant and eat a huge frozen custard for me."

Stupor gave a thumbs up as Vengence's gaze shifted toward the guards. He gave Stupor a final glance and stood up.

Vengence began walking toward the exit as Stupor looked forward, innocently twiddling his thumbs and humming. Halfway there, Vengence detected movement in the corner of his eye. He looked over and saw a nurse moving within the void that separated Stupor from all the other inmates. She wore a medical mask that hid her face and held a syringe in one hand.

Vengence watched as she approached Stupor from behind, stepping lightly as if she did not want to be detected.

Vengence briskly approached the nurse and shoved her hard, knocking her down to the floor.

Stupor jumped in his chair at the nearby sound and whipped around to see all the commotion. Vengence's actions instantly alerted the guards, who began to move toward him quickly.

"You may now consider us even, Baron Von Stupor," Vengence said to Stupor while pointing at the nurse. "This woman was going to kill you."

Stupor immediately looked at the nurse, who stared back at him with terrified eyes. He looked at the syringe that had dropped from her hand and saw it filled entirely with what he could only assume was anesthesia. The nurse quickly got up and ran away, leaving the syringe behind.

Stupor looked back at Vengence in time to see him smash a second guard's head into a table and take his stun baton. Vengence then barreled out of the common room and into the kitchen. Soon after only crashing could be heard.

I wish I had the guts to do something like that, Stupor thought to himself.

My foolish generosity may have cost me my only chance to escape! Vengence thought as he ran with all his might through the kitchen exit and across the courtyard toward the security building.

Looking around him, he saw security guards running at him from all directions, stun batons in hand.

Vengence entered the covered walkway and approached the building's metal door, key card in hand.

"This had better work," Vengence said aloud, swiping the card.

The lock made a pleasant chirping sound as it unlocked. Vengence yanked the door open and rushed inside to see Lanzendorf emerge from the administrative hallway, holding a shotgun.

"Well if it isn't the jolly green giant," he said, pointing the gun at Vengence.

"Your lack of honor disgusts me," he growled back, leering.

"Honor is a thing of the past, you bald idiot. Everything is simply a means to an end."

"I will die before I submit to your shame!"

Vengence ran at Lanzendorf, who wasted no time firing the gun. Vengence instantly reeled back as a bean bag smashed him square in the chest. He hunched over and roared in pain as the sharp, searing sensation rang throughout his body. He then furiously looked back up and saw Lanzendorf's face had changed from confidence to utter fright.

Vengence angrily tore after Lanzendorf, who scrambled back into the administrative hallway. After entering, Lanzendorf slammed the door behind him and continued down the hallway toward his office.

Before Vengence could get into the hallway, security guards erupted from inside. He looked behind and noticed that the guards following him had rounded the corner he came from.

Vengence charged into the crowd, thrashing as wildly as he could. He was easily overwhelmed by the sheer number of guards, however, and was once again sedated.

***

"Hello, good sir doctor," Stupor greeted, as he somberly came into Dr. Goodrich's office. He plodded over to the office's desk and plopped in a chair, sulking.

"That entrance was less-than-energetic. Most certainly not your style," the doctor observed.

"Oh, I suppose I feel pretty normal today," Stupor responded, looking down at the floor. "I mean, I was able to make a new friend recently, which is amazing. I don't know if you know, but his name is Vengence."

"Patient C26 won't be joining us anymore after today."

Stupor looked up at Dr. Goodrich.

"He got a healthy release?" he asked, hopeful.

"I'm not at liberty to discuss other patients with you, I'm sorry."

Stupor sat back in his seat and grumpily crossed his arms.

"It seems like something is really bothering you," the doctor prodded. "Why don't we talk about it?" Receiving no response, he sat back and interlaced his fingers, relaxing. "How about we play a simple game? If I correctly guess what is bothering you, we move on with our session and talk about it."

Stupor glanced over at Dr. Goodrich without saying a word.

"I'm willing to bet..." the doctor continued,

taking a short pause to choose his words. "...that you're upset about patient C26 no longer being here anymore."

"Is it illegal to talk about that?" Stupor asked.

"Depends. Is that what is bothering you?"

"Not having my new friend around anymore bothers me a lot."

"That's very understandable. Unfortunately, it's highly unlikely he'll return as well. He's going to be transferred to a crisis unit."

Stupor jumped in his chair on hearing this.

"Oh no, Vengence!" he exclaimed.

After his initial reaction, Stupor slumped in his chair and sadly looked to the floor again. He breathed a heavy sigh as the doctor continued to watch him.

"What I'd like to know, however, is how this turn of events is bothering you if you never could have known it unless it came through me," Dr. Goodrich stated, leaning forward and resting his arms on the table.

"Well, Vengence going to a crisis unit is news to me," Stupor responded half-heartedly.

"Yes, and yet you somehow knew about him leaving the asylum, crisis unit or no crisis unit. Stupor, were you helping him escape?"

Stupor shrugged his shoulders and said to the doctor, "I only know he left because you told me. I said it bothers me, I didn't say it bothered me before I got here. And I still think that you telling me that stuff is illegal."

Dr. Goodrich gave Stupor a flat stare and

began writing on a sheet of paper from his file.

"It always seems like you write on the same pieces of paper during our sessions. Where do you find the room?" Stupor asked, watching him.

"Let's talk about your name," Dr. Goodrich flatly suggested, ignoring his question. "How did you get the name 'Baron Von Stupor'?"

"But–"

"Please tell me how you got your name."

"Well if you have to know, it's kind of a weird story, so try not to think I'm making this up. I was eating some alphabet soup once as a wee child. I lifted my spoon and there in it were letters, spelling the word 'HELP'.

"'I shall do no such thing!' I cried aloud, and threw the spoon.

"The soup's impetuousness outraged me so much that I smacked the bowl with all my might! However, I missed and the tips of my fingers hit it instead. That really smarted!

"The bowl spilled off the table and I held my hand, crying 'alack!' As I wept aloud I noticed the letters scattered all over the floor. On closer inspection, they spelled out a haunting message: 'THAT IS WHAT YOU GET FOR BEING SO MEAN BARON VON STUPOR'.

"With this newfound revelation of my true identity, I made a vow to myself that if I were to ever have help requested of me by an inanimate object, I certainly would oblige it! The end."

"And the V?" Dr. Goodrich asked without reaction, writing on his paper.

"Well, there were no lowercase noodles and I didn't know any better because I was young. It just kinda stuck after that."

Dr. Goodrich continued to write for a few moments. On finishing, he impatiently slapped the pen down and waved his hand dismissively.

"We're done," he said. "Go see Michala to schedule our next session."

"Seems like something's bothering you. "Do you wanna talk about it?" Stupor asked, feeling a bit more livened.

"Go away," he snapped back.

Shrugging his shoulders, Stupor got up and left the room.

***

Lanzendorf calmly stepped into the office of Dr. Perez and shut the door behind him.

"Hello, Mr. Lanzendorf," she greeted with a neutral expression on her face. "What can I do for you?"

She turned away from her bookshelf and approached her chair, standing behind it.

"Dr. Perez, I'm glad you asked," Lanzendorf responded, approaching her desk.

He looked about the office, quietly scoffing the careful effort put into its interior design. The walls were lined with various awards and degrees, an analog clock located within eyeshot of her chair. Behind her desk sat a bookshelf with all kinds of medical journals and reference books.

The desk itself was kept neat and orderly, yet personalized with a picture of herself and her husband.

Dr. Perez had stopped what she was doing and continued to look at Lanzendorf, expecting him to talk.

"I have something very important that I need you to do," he informed her with a smug grin.

"Please, Mr. Lanzendorf, what do you want? I'm really busy."

"It's really rather simple," he stated, leaning on her desk with one hand. "I want you to make sure that patient C26 does not get transferred to another institution."

Dr. Perez looked at him with surprised eyes. Without breaking eye contact, she took a few moments to process what had been asked of her.

"Are you serious? That patient is extremely dangerous and cannot get appropriate care here."

"Oh, I am absolutely serious. This facility is completely capable of giving him proper 'care', he just needs some more time and more of my brand of persuasion."

"He would have taken your head clean off if it weren't for your staff," she reminded him with an irritated stare.

"I didn't need my staff to handle him! I was trained by the best of the best in the military. I've killed people more dangerous than him with my bare hands."

"I don't understand why you'd even want someone like him to stay here."

"The reason I want him to stay is because we've had dangerous men here before, and my security procedures have turned them all into pussycats! This is a perfect facility, and a perfect facility can handle any inmate, no matter how big, strong, or scary."

"That man is far more dangerous than any patient in the history of the wellness center," Dr. Perez argued, narrowing her eyes in disapproval. "There is no way I'll support him staying."

"I think you will," Lanzendorf insisted. "That is, unless you want upper management to find out about your annoying little Vicodin problem. I can bring it up anytime, you know."

Dr. Perez's mood sank as Lanzendorf's smile broadened slightly. She felt her posture melting uncontrollably.

"Why are you always doing this to me?" she asked, her shoulders slouched. "Why does it have to always come back to that?"

"I'm merely doing what anyone else would do when in passionate pursuit of their interests. It's nothing personal; I just want what I want and you're in my way."

"I hate you so much."

"And I hate failure," Lanzendorf said over his shoulder as he walked to the exit. "So surely you understand how upset I might be if patient C26 is transferred out of my perfect facility."

Lanzendorf took his leave as Dr. Perez sat down at her desk and wiped at her watering eyes.

***

"B256," called a security guard, approaching him in the common room. "Come with me; you have visitors."

"Alright!" yipped Stupor, swinging his arm and scampering to meet the guard. "They're here pretty late."

"You're gonna have to make it sort of quick since the reception area is trying to shut down for the evening," the guard informed him.

Stupor was escorted across the courtyard and into the reception building. He bouncily stepped into the visitor's lobby and briefly admired the décor he saw less often than he would prefer.

The floor had a yellow and blue checker-patterned carpet and vibrant white walls. There were gorgeous oil on canvas paintings decorating the walls and a gas fireplace integrated into the far end of the visitor's lobby. Stupor couldn't help but feel like the room might be a bit larger than necessary for the number of visitors that came through simultaneously.

At one of the many small tables in the room sat Stupor's adoptive parents, Harry and Jane Aikens. Harry was a laid back man, though very successful financially. Jane had always been more of a stay-at-home mom, giving them a somewhat clichéd existence.

Harry stood at Stupor's height, with lightly grayed brown hair kept combed straight back. He was a thin man, yet healthy for his age of 55. He appeared to have come straight from work as he still wore his white collar work outfit.

Jane dressed much more casually, sporting a simple pair of jeans and a dark violet hoodie. Her short blonde hair was nicely parted to one side.

"Wow, you guys sure picked a heck of a day to visit me!" he chirped as he jogged ahead of the security guard to sit down in a chair. "Today's been pretty crappy."

"I'm sorry to hear that," Harry said to him with a light smile. "What happened?"

"I finally managed to make a new friend, but then he beat up a bunch of people and got in trouble. Now I hear he's gonna be transferred out."

"Um... That's too bad," Jane consoled, giving Harry a mildly uncomfortable look. "What was his name?"

"He wouldn't tell anyone, so I named him Baron Von Poorly Spelled Vengence. We really had a lot in common, so it sucks that he's gone!"

"Common?" Harry uttered involuntarily.

"Oh, yes indeed," Stupor replied obliviously. "We both felt like we don't belong here, and we both would love to get out sometime soon."

"Stupor, why aren't you wearing your normal clothes?" Harry asked uncomfortably, not quite catching Stupor's entire response.

"Oh, I lost that privilege about a day ago because they think I started a riot."

His parents' eyes widened with surprise. They

looked at each other for a moment, then back to him.

"Wh-what do you mean you started a riot?" Jane asked Stupor, sounding slightly panicked.

"Well, I didn't actually start it. I was playing a rousing game of Tag with Vengence and then he accidentally picked Booby up over his head and accidentally threw him straight at another group of patients. Total accident, of course. I tried to stop the other patients from beating Vengence up. I think I was moderately successful!"

"Honey, what happened to you? You used to be doing so well here!"

"Pretty much the fact that Vengence had to leave. I was extremely okay until that happened."

"What she means is that you used to try," Harry chimed in. "You used to cooperate with the staff. You used to try to get better so you can come home. Now you're just causing trouble and fighting with people."

"I thought you guys wanted me to be more social? You're just never happy, are you?" Stupor asked with his hands on his hips.

His parents sat flabbergasted for a moment, whereupon Stupor laughed to himself. "That was a joke," he informed them. "But seriously, I feel fine. When am I going to get out of here?"

"How can you sit right there thinking this is funny?" his father asked, becoming impatient. "You being in here is very hard for us and you're treating everything like it's just some big joke. I picked up your mother and came straight here after work. I'm tired as hell and you're going to laugh about starting a riot and then ask when you're getting out? What happened to you since the last time we visited you?"

"Realistically speaking, the riot's the only real difference between now and the last time you visited me," Stupor corrected him. "But with that aside, I really don't blame you guys. I know you care about me and stuff. It's just that cooperating didn't get me anywhere. No matter how hard I try, people just won't believe me when I try to tell them about the courtroom. So what's the point? I'm just having fun when I can and when I get out, I get out."

"You're never going to get out thinking like that," his mother interjected. "The sooner you come to terms with the courtroom incident, the better."

"It's hard to come to terms with it if I wasn't there," Stupor responded casually, shrugging his shoulders.

"Who attacked the magistrate, then?" his dad asked, raising his voice. "Who wore your mask? Who did I see jump up with his hands cuffed, roundhouse the bailiff, do some crazy acrobatics I've never seen before, and then land a foot clean into the face of the magistrate?"

"A roundhouse? I'd say it was Chuck Norris," Stupor insisted, unfazed. "But it's really hard to think of anything for sure since I wasn't even there."

"Chuck Norris," Harry muttered under his

breath before standing up and pacing away with his hand over his mouth.

"Harry, calm down," Jane sternly told him.

"How can I? How can I, dear?" he spat as he whipped back around. "Everything else, I could deal with. The Watcher? Or the Kanghoulroo? Harmless.

"Then he kicks a magistrate—his magistrate. And now he started a riot. This is insanity! He's getting worse, and I'm going to have a nice talk with one of the directors here about it."

Noticing the increased tension, the security guard stepped forward and approached them.

"I'm going to have to cut the visit a little bit short," he announced to them. "Emotions seem to be getting heated and we need to lock down the building anyway."

"That's fine, I understand," Harry said to the guard. He then turned back to Stupor. "Son, I'm sorry for getting so upset. However, you need to cooperate with the staff. You need to work on getting better and the first step is remembering what really happened in that courtroom."

"I stopped cooperating when I realized that nobody is on my side," Stupor said to them in a somber tone. "Nobody except Vengence and he's gone now."

Stupor then quietly hugged his family and left to return to his cell.

***

"I won't take long," Mr. Bark said aloud to the other directors in the board meeting room. "However, I'm sure we can all understand this is something that requires immediate attention."

"We don't require a meeting," Dr. Goodrich said. "That man has to go."

"I-I'd like to discuss the matter a bit further, actually," Dr. Perez spoke with hesitation.

"He is too dangerous for this facility. He has hurt people, attempted escape, and even attacked Mr. Lanzendorf. Exactly what is there to discuss?" Dr. Goodrich ranted.

"Progress," she replied. "We've managed to establish a social relationship, even if it's through one of the other patients."

"Stupor is using C26 as a pawn and nothing more."

"But it's progress nonetheless, and I feel like Dr. Goodrich may be partially biased due to his own inability to connect with the patient the way Stupor has."

Dr. Goodrich's expression snapped to one of insult and bafflement.

"I think no matter where patient C26 goes, things are only going to get worse before they get better," Mr. Jenkins chimed in. "I say we keep C26 under better control and wait a bit longer. At least long enough to get some testing results."

"I agree," Dr. Perez added. "I am not saying he should go or stay, I'm saying we need some results before we can really make a firm decision. After some examination, we may even be able to settle him down with some kind of medication plan."

"This is ridiculous!" Dr. Goodrich objected. "I am the psychiatrist in this facility and it seems like you're all baselessly rejecting my professional opinions!"

"Dr. Goodrich, your professional opinion is invaluable, but it seems like everything you're saying may be stained with your personal feelings about Stupor," Mr. Bark said to him.

"My personal feelings have nothing to do with my suspicions about his scheming!"

"I think they do. I would like to add that even Mr. Lanzendorf advocated C26 staying in the facility despite his disposition of Stupor."

"People are getting hurt," Mr. Ritzo argued. "That should be the bottom line. People are getting hurt and he needs to go."

"We deal with dangerous people every day," Mr. Jenkins retaliated. "We eat and work around them. Sometimes we socialize with them. The chance of getting hurt comes with the position, especially for security. If you're not comfortable with that, Sean, then you need to take a moment to reconsider your job."

"That's enough," Mr. Bark interjected. "Let's just vote so we can get this all over with and go home for the day. Who is in favor of C26 being transferred to another facility?"

Mr. Ritzo and Dr. Goodrich looked around the room, raising their hands with heavy frowns. The other directors sat awkwardly as Mr. Bark let out a heavy sigh.

"Well, it seems this motion has been denied and patient C26 will be allowed to continue his treatment here," he announced as he stood up.

"This is absolutely ridiculous," Dr. Goodrich grunted as he rose from the table in a huff. "You are all ridiculous!"

***

Stupor entered his cell and immediately climbed up to his bunk. Jörg was already in bed on the bottom.

"You awake?" Stupor asked him.

"Ja," he lazily replied.

"My parents came to visit me today. The conversation went back to the courtroom again. Seems to be a trending topic. It makes me enjoy their visits less."

"Du wirst eines Tages zerbrechen," he calmly responded. "Dann wirst du verstehen, genau wie ich an dem Tag, an dem ich mich von meinen Eltern befreit habe."

"I mean, I understand where they're coming from; it really looks like I'm the one that did it! But I'd never hurt someone like that. In my heart it feels like I didn't do it."

"Das Herz betrügt die Menschen. Die Augen betrügen die Menschen. Eines Tages wirst du genau erfahren, wie falsch unser aller Sinne sind."

"Except for Vengence, I think you're the only

person here who actually likes to talk to me. I just wish I knew what the heck you're saying!"

To this, Jörg chuckled and responded, "Vertrau mir, du möchtest die Dinge nicht wissen, die ich weiß. Die sind genau der Grund, warum ich hier bin."

"I'm gonna go to sleep now, Jörg. Thanks for always listening to me."

Stupor rolled over in his bed and shut his eyes. It was a bit difficult, but before too long he managed to drift into slumber.

***

"Mankind has a price to pay."

Chapter Seven

Stupor woke up and looked about his room, confused. He then hopped out of his bed and saw Jörg standing just outside the cell door.

"Jörg! Do you wanna know how to wake up appreciating life?" he asked the cellmate.

Jörg gave Stupor a quizzical look.

"You dream about Oprah Winfrey exposing you via television for crimes you committed and being put under military arrest! I totally thought I was done for!"

Jörg looked completely confused.

"Oh, don't worry; in my dream I technically committed them, but it was for the benefit of mankind! No malice was intended."

The two stared at each other in silence. After a few moments, Stupor gave Jörg a quick double thumbs up and waddled away, uttering "blub, blub, blub".

On entering the common room, he drew a deep breath and looked around. *Vengence isn't here anymore, but I can't let that keep me down!* he thought to himself. *My happiness is the only thing that keeps me sane here!*

He then noticed a void in the center of the room with a large security presence observing it. Weaving around a few people, he noticed an all-too-familiar face sitting in the void's center, his head lying down on his arms.

"Vengence, I can't believe you're still here!" Stupor squealed as he hippity-hopped over to his table, his fists pumping in the air. "Man, I totally thought you were done for!"

Vengence glanced at Stupor without turning his head and took a deep breath.

"What do you want?" he asked Stupor.

"I'd like to know your real name, actually! Is it Chuck?"

"Leave me alone."

"You're probably just cranky since you didn't escape. Here, I have something that will cheer you up!"

Stupor then reached underneath his mask and extracted a key card. Discretely, he sat down at Vengence's table and slipped it underneath his arms.

Vengence subtly grasped the card with his hand and gave Stupor a distrustful look.

"Where do you keep getting these?" he asked.

"Where do you think I keep getting them?" Stupor replied with a snorting chuckle.

"You did not even know I would be here. Do you collect these under that mask?"

Stupor casually shrugged his shoulders and shot Vengence a thumbs up before standing.

"Your sneakiness makes me very suspicious, boy," Vengence told him, sitting up. "Why do you not try to escape if you are so boldly intent on helping me?"

"I've seen how far you can get with all your superpowers. I obviously can't escape on my own, but I figure that maybe if we work together at least one of us will get the freedom we deserve."

"This is an insane asylum. How exactly are you wrongly here?"

"I say shenanigans, but your guess is as good as mine."

Vengence rolled his eyes and looked toward the guards, paying particular attention to Officer Abernathy. Abernathy smirked back, patting his stun baton while the guards adjacent to him shifted their weight uncomfortably.

Vengence held back his anger, balling up his fists and snarling. He then looked down at his open hand to see his key card inadvertently crushed. Before he could react, another key card plopped down on the table in front of him.

Vengence confusedly looked back up at Stupor, who shrugged his shoulders. Without wasting another moment, Stupor walked away toward the tray pick-up window for breakfast.

Abernathy caught a tiny glimpse of Vengence holding the key card and sharply ordered the guards forward.

"C26, show me your hands now," Abernathy commanded from behind the wall of guards.

"Step in front of your meat shield and make me, Terran," Vengence demanded.

"Show me your hands!" Abernathy repeated, stubbornly refusing to approach. Vengence sat in quiet refusal, staring at him.

"Okay everyone, you know what to do. Let's get some restraints on him," Abernathy coolly instructed the guards.

They all looked at each other uncomfortably.

"Did anyone hear me? Put him in restraints right now!" Abernathy repeated impatiently.

"With all due respect," spoke Officer Herald from the others. "He's not attacking anyone and I think I speak for all of us when I say we don't feel like getting hurt. I feel like there's a much better way to approach this than conflict."

"But I'm the lead officer!" Abernathy angrily declared. "Unless you guys want to be written up, I suggest you restrain him!"

Herald leered at Abernathy critically, turning away from Vengence. "You're not the lead officer anymore, Guy," he reminded him. "You just got demoted, remember? I'm telling you I personally do not feel comfortable provoking patient C26 and I'm not going to do it."

Officer Herald shot Abernathy a dirty look and walked away. As Abernathy glared back at Herald, he could hear an audible chuckle from Vengence.

"Isn't anyone going to restrain this goon?!" Abernathy asked the other guards.

One by one, the guards returned to their old posts, leaving only Abernathy behind. Abernathy turned and looked down at Vengence's wry grin.

"And then there was one," he said with a hint of wryness. "Run away, little man. Or do you challenge me to Honorable Resolution?"

Abernathy looked at him with gritted teeth and stormed off. He blew past the other guards and left the common room.

Stupor approached Vengence with his tray

and sat down at the table. "Wow," he said. "The fact that they didn't restrain you is surprising."

"If they are smart, they will reset the card scanners," Vengence commented.

In a moment of realization, Stupor snapped his fingers and leaned close to Vengence. "Hey, what did you mean when you were talking about that one nurse trying to kill me?" he asked.

"You would know better than I," Vengence responded. "You are the one she is trying to kill."

"Why would anyone ever want me dead? I'm really confused."

"You should ask her. She was in this room earlier."

Stupor felt a chill roll down his spine.

"Of course you would not know," Vengence scoffed. "Terran civilians are so vulnerable."

Stupor looked around the room carefully, analyzing the nurses' faces.

"She watches you often," Vengence informed him. "If she had not tried to kill you, I would have suspected her to be lecherous."

"I wish you'd have told me about her a whole lot sooner," Stupor muttered.

"I barely recognized you as a competent life form before today."

Stupor futilely continued watching for her. "I don't see her anywhere..." he complained. "Can you find her for me?"

"Find her yourself," Vengence snapped. "The information I have provided to you makes our debts even once more. Do not expect any further generosity from me."

"What? Come on!" Stupor begged, becoming increasingly nervous. "This is basically a life or death situation for me!"

"Good. Perhaps after dealing with it, you will become more of a man."

"T-that's not fair!" Stupor sputtered, standing up. "I'm gonna go and ask someone else for help, because I like being alive!"

"You Terrans have little concept of bravery." Vengence jeered. "You are nothing but spineless cowards that seek to hide behind one another."

"Well, this spineless coward can't get you any more key cards if he's dead!" Stupor said over his shoulder while briskly walking away.

He noticed Lanzendorf enter the room with an irritated frown on his face. He set his eyes on Vengence and began to approach quickly. Stupor noticed this and swiftly intercepted him.

"Mr. Lanzendorf, I need your help," he earnestly said.

Lanzendorf shoved Stupor away without any hesitation and continued on his warpath. A few strides later, he stopped and turned slowly, giving Stupor a confused look.

"You... what?" he asked, stumbling over his words.

"You may find this really hard to believe, Mr. Lanzendorf, but I think someone's trying to kill me."

Lanzendorf gave a brief skeptical look before flashing a smug grin. "I don't believe you at all," he said. "You are an insane asylum patient with violence and hallucinations in your history. Why on Earth should I believe you?"

"Video evidence, maybe?" Stupor answered with a shrug of his shoulders. "You don't even have to take my word for it. If you look back at Vengence's escape attempt, you'll see some nurse coming toward me with a syringe all sneaky-like. Don't you think that would be kinda weird?"

Lanzendorf furrowed his brows and looked off to one side in thought.

"Mr. Lanzendorf, we don't get along well and that's a fact," Stupor added. "But grudges aside, I'm pretty sure you wouldn't want me dead. You don't have to do anything now, but can you at least look at that video tape and use your best professional judgment?"

"I really should," he uttered to himself under his breath.

"Vengence told me she watches me a lot," Stupor continued. "And she was here earlier."

"C26? Why don't you have him protect you instead of bothering me?"

"He won't do it! He says dealing with a life or death situation will make me more of a man. I say I like staying alive, and that's why I need your help. You're the only person here that absolutely needs me alive to accomplish their goal, because you can't break the spirit of a dead man."

After another moment of intense thought, Lanzendorf gave a heavy sigh and said, "Fine. Go see Officer Herald at the door and I'll have him take you to an isolation chamber."

"Meh, isolation," Stupor whined.

"It's for safety!" Lanzendorf snapped, his face flashing with anger. He then jabbed his finger at Stupor sternly and added, "And I swear, you had better hope I'm not wasting my time with a delusional snipe hunt or I'll be the one holding that syringe."

Lanzendorf then walked away, speaking to Officer Herald before leaving the room. Officer Herald nodded his head in acknowledgment and approached Stupor.

"Come with me and we'll get you into an isolation chamber," he instructed.

A very relieved Stupor was then escorted to the security building by Herald.

***

Lanzendorf approached the CCTV room and found Officer Abernathy inside, monitoring the cameras.

"I thought Wilson had CCTV duty today?" he asked him.

"I switched posts with him; he's going to take over my spot in the common room," Abernathy replied, looking over his shoulder at Lanzendorf.

"I need you to pull the footage from C26's escape attempt yesterday," Lanzendorf instructed, dismissing Abernathy's reasoning. "Show me the common room."

Without a word, Abernathy looked into the

asylum's security video archives and opened the appropriate video file. After sifting through the footage for a few minutes, they came across the feed that was recorded just before Vengence's escape attempt.

Lanzendorf tapped his chin inquisitively, watching the black and white feed. His eyes slowly widened as he watched Vengence break from his path to quickly push the approaching nurse over. He watched the footage multiple times for confirmation.

"What... the... hell...?" Abernathy exclaimed. "She's even creeping along like she's trying to be quiet."

"I'll be damned. B256 might be half right about someone trying to kill him," Lanzendorf said. "It's too fuzzy for me to really see her well, though. Just medium length black hair."

"Why didn't she delete the security footage, though? If she wants him dead, she should be more careful about it. She's an idiot."

"Idiot or not, she wouldn't be able to delete the footage because it's saved to another off-site location. We can access the footage, but we can't delete anything due to some computer crap. That at least explains why she would wear the medical mask."

"So... what do we do, sir?"

Lanzendorf stood up straight but refused to break his gaze from the computer screens. "I have B256 safe in an isolation chamber for now," he informed Abernathy. "You watch the cameras for anyone that remotely looks like that woman. I'm going to visit the medical building and speak to our dear Dr. Perez."

"Do you really think it was her?" Abernathy asked, eyebrows raised.

"I'd say she's more of a person of interest at this point."

***

"What do you want now, Mr. Lanzendorf?" Dr. Perez impatiently asked as he shut her office door behind him.

"Right now I'm just gathering information," Lanzendorf informed her. "Doctor, where were you yesterday?"

"Why would you care?" she snapped. "If you don't have some legitimate business, then get out."

"My business here is more than legitimate. I have reason to believe that someone here wants patient B256 dead. Now tell me where you've been yesterday."

She stared at Lanzendorf in surprise. "What? Why haven't you—" she began.

"Just answer my goddamn question, Perez!" Lanzendorf shouted, completely cutting her off cold. "Where were you yesterday?!"

Dr. Perez recoiled slightly from his outburst, then retaliated with impatience.

"I was taking my son to baseball practice!" she lashed, raising her voice. "I came in for the emergency meeting and that was all! Now tell me what I have to do with any of this and why you haven't called the police!"

"I'll make that call when I deem it necessary. Right now, I'm simply gathering information. So apparently, there was a woman with medium-length black hair who appears to have attempted the murder of patient B256 yesterday. She was dressed as a nurse and wore a medical mask to conceal her face."

"What exactly are you insinuating? You think I could have done it?"

Lanzendorf narrowed his eyes and stared at Dr. Perez. "I'm not going to make accusations," he said to her in a low tone. "However, a few things I do know about the medical building is that there are only four females that work in it and you are the only one that has medium-length black hair."

Dr. Perez glared at him with a quiet rage. Her face flushed as her blood boiled. "I'm calling the police so they can handle it," she angrily asserted and picked up her phone.

"If you value your job, you'll put that phone down and keep your goddamn nose out of this," Lanzendorf said loudly.

Dr. Perez squeezed the phone and continued to stare daggers. "I don't even have motive," she spat. "I care about all of our patients and have no reason to want to hurt any of them. The fact that you would even suggest it is just idiotic."

"Actually, *Erika*, you do have a motive," he

said with stabbing disrespect. "It's to get back at me. I could involve the police, but then I might just lose my trump card for board meetings. I just want time to make sure I have my ducks in a row before I give that up."

Lanzendorf turned to leave the office. As he exited, he spoke over his shoulder, "I suggest you keep your ducks in a row too. If you're trying to screw me over, I'll find out. And then I'll ruin everything you've ever held dear."

As he shut the door behind him, he saw Mr. Ritzo standing outside his office door, watching him while wearing a harsh frown of disapproval. Lanzendorf shot him a dirty look before leaving the building.

***

Stupor lay wide awake on the small bed in his isolation chamber. He rolled over roughly, impatient from restlessness. Suddenly, his door opened and Officer Abernathy stood before him.

"Hello, good sir!" he greeted the guard.

"Don't talk to me like I owe you anything," Abernathy nastily responded. "I'm just helping you because it's part of my job."

"Oh, I'm sorry," Stupor apologized. "I was unaware that greetings implied some sort of debt. I will instead dance in response to your presence and hopefully that will–"

"That's enough B256," Abernathy cut him off. "Get out. It's time for your group therapy."

"You can at least let a guy finish a joke," he muttered while stepping out of the chamber. "So what about my wannabe murderer?"

"Mr. Lanzendorf's been investigating for a while and he can't figure anything out. He said to keep you on schedule and we're going to keep a close watch on you in case that woman comes back."

Stupor scratched his head and asked, "Well, why not call the police? This is a rather serious matter."

"That's his business, not mine. Get out and a guard will escort you to your therapy session."

That guy probably just doesn't want to risk me being transferred out of here, Stupor thought to himself. *You can always count on good old William 'Come-Hell-or-High-Water' Lanzendorf...*

Stupor was escorted from his cell to Dr. Goodrich's building and a guard then stood inside to monitor the session. As Stupor found his seat, his escort found a place among the several other guards that monitored Vengence.

"Alright everyone," Dr. Goodrich announced to the therapy group attendees. "We have a new patient with us, so I'd like to give him a warm welcome." Looking at a sheet of paper in his hand, he said, "Let's give a friendly welcome to, uh..."

Dr. Goodrich trailed off and examined the paper closely, appearing a bit bewildered. "Baron Von Poorly Spelled Vengence? Is this some kind of joke?" he asked, looking at Stupor.

"I can assure you," Stupor chuckled, pointing at Vengence. "That is indeed his name!"

"It is not my name," Vengence voiced sternly and gestured toward Stupor. "This idiot is the one responsible for that humiliating label."

"Hm. I'll certainly look into that," the doctor said, giving Stupor a highly suspicious glare. "In the meantime, we can start with an introduction from you, then." Dr. Goodrich sat in his chair and gestured to Vengence. "Feel free to formally share your actual name to the group and tell us a little about yourself."

Vengence stood up and looked down at the patients in contempt. "I will not tell you my name," he spat. "I will not tell you my past. I will not share with you any details you cannot discern by looking at me. This entire group fills me with disgust and that man looks like a fighter pilot." Vengence then pointed directly at Terry, who appeared thoroughly surprised and offended.

"Who do you think you are, calling me a fighter pilot, huh?!" Terry shot at him angrily. His anger was short-lived as he slowly realized how inoffensive Vengence's comment was. "You think that I'm some kind of pilot that, uh... flies jets and... shoots at stuff?"

"Flying jets would be the only use you have in this world, you diminutive Terran," Vengence uttered before sitting back down. He folded his arms and looked off toward the fireplace.

Terry simply looked back at him, perplexed. He sat in his chair and struggled to make sense of Vengence's words. As he thought to himself, everyone else remained silent.

"You're the first person to make a comment that Terry couldn't be offended by," a patient named Kate observed.

Kate Harris was a young woman who had herself committed a little over a month ago. She suffered from a deep depression after having her heart broken by a man younger than her. She stands at five and a half feet and keeps her long, scarlet red hair very well-maintained. She wears medical scrubs at the facility's behest as she is considered a danger to herself.

Stupor energetically clapped his hands at her statement as everyone awkwardly watched him. "I tried to tell you how awesome Vengence is and he proved it just now!" Stupor praised him.

"Shut up," Vengence muttered in response.

"You got it, pal!"

Seeking progress, Dr. Goodrich stood up and grabbed a nearby top hat. He pulled out a small handful of paper scraps and pens and began to move about the circle.

"Well," he said. "It's perfectly fine if, uh... Vengence doesn't wish to share his real name. I suppose, then, that we should move on to our pre-therapy game. We won't be playing 'Mimic' anymore due to patients' abuse of the game's freedom; we'll instead play a game called 'Ask It Basket'."

Dr. Goodrich then began explaining the game as he distributed scraps of paper and pens to everyone. "For this game, I would like you all to write down your strongest negative emotion. We'll then take all of those emotions and place them into my top hat. After that, volunteers may come up and pick a paper scrap from the hat and share experiences with that particular emotion."

Dr. Goodrich collected the scraps and stirred them up vigorously in the hat. He then extracted a single scrap out and looked at it.

"Just so it's fair, I will take the first turn," he declared with a light smile and held the scrap up for everyone to see. "I drew 'fear'. My experience with this emotion can be a bit humorous. You see, I actually suffer from ichthyophobia, which is an irrational fear of fish.

"It all started when I was a young child. My father had a friend who owned an old trawling vessel. Well, my father had me standing on the edge of the tray where the fish were. One of them jumped up at me and spooked me.

"Next thing I knew, I slipped and fell right into the pile of fish. I felt all the slimy scales as they slipped all around me. My father pulled me out pretty quickly, but not before I got a few stings from the little thorns they have under their fins.

"Now, I know that was just one time and that fish are mostly harmless, but that one experience is the only thing that comes to mind whenever I see a fish and I become absolutely terrified."

"Pathetic," Vengence grunted, eliciting a look of disapproval from Dr. Goodrich.

“Now then, who would like to go next?” the doctor asked, shaking the top hat vigorously.

Stupor’s hand immediately shot into the air. Dr. Goodrich gave him a critical look before glancing around the room. He then released a defeated sigh and called on Stupor.

“All right!” he chirped, strolling over to the hat and pulling a paper out. “I got ‘deception’, so here goes! How many of you love to sit with a nice Sham sandwich with mustard? Oh man, I love it! Well, have you ever been to the official Sham Museum? It’s a really cool place! However, there’s things about the production of Sham that the factory doesn’t want you to know about! I know this because I went there.

“So I go into the factory one day on a tour and I looked up at the production line. There was a pig standing on an empty can of Sham. Suddenly, a piston came out of nowhere and totally smashed the entire pig into the can!”

The group recoiled in complete disgust while Dr. Goodrich furrowed his brows. He opened his mouth to speak, but Stupor had already resumed talking.

“Well okay, it wasn’t the whole pig,” Stupor continued. “Its head was sticking out of the can still. And that’s when the piston came down a second time and smashed the pig’s head into the can!”

“That doesn’t really make any sense…” Terry said, challenging Stupor’s story.

“Actually… hold on. Terry, I agree,” Stupor

mentioned, thinking. "It doesn't seem right. You know what, I think that was actually just a dream I had a long time ago! But I tell you, I still woke up feeling pretty deceived!"

The patients groaned as the frustrated doctor massaged his temples. "Stupor, please sit down," he asked, struggling to contain his impatience.

"I hope you all learned a valuable lesson from all of this," Stupor commented as he sat.

"Patient C26, would you like to go next?" the doctor asked him, extending the hat toward him.

"Negative," Vengence flatly refused without looking in his direction.

Jörg raised his hand and smiled. Not seeing any other hands raised, he sighed and held out the hat to Jörg.

***

As Stupor's cell door was locked behind him, he immediately began talking to his bunkmate, who sat at the desk.

"Jörg, I have some super crazy news for you," Stupor told him. "I think someone's trying to kill me!"

Jörg gave Stupor a skeptical look.

"I managed to convince Mr. Lanzendorf, so it's gotta be partially true," he continued. "I just wish I knew why someone would want me dead."

Jörg stood up, excited, and patted Stupor on his back. "Wenn jemand versucht mich zu töten, fühle ich mich am lebendigsten," he said, giving a big nod of approval. "Du solltest sehr glücklich sein, mein Freund!"

"No, Jörg, I want to stay alive. This is really serious!" Stupor corrected him, climbing into his bunk. "Someone wants me dead, and I want to live."

"Bah," Jörg replied, waving Stupor away. He rolled into his bunk and watched the wall.

"It might not be so bad to you, but it means a lot to me! I act silly outside the cell still, but I'm honestly pretty scared," Stupor admitted, staring at the ceiling. "And the more I think about it, the more nervous I get. Like what if she tries to come in the cell and kill me?"

"Du hast nichts zu fürchten. Wenn ich es wäre, der versuchen würde, dich zu töten, dann hättest du ein Problem."

"Jörg, I don't know what I'd do without your support. I know I say it too much, but thanks for hearing me out!"

"Wir sind beste Freunde und unsere Freundschaft wird sogar noch wachsen, sobald du deine wahre Bestimmung erkennst."

Stupor rolled over and with effort, finally fell asleep.

***

"POTATOPOTATOPOTATOPOTATOPOTATO POTATOPOTATOPOTATOPOTATOPOTATOP OTATOPOTATOPOTATOPOTATOPOTATO"

****

Vengence looked at the clock and saw the time was nearly ten at night.

"The time seems just about right," he said to himself, rolling off of his drooping bed.

Vengence then stuck his finger far into his mouth, causing a self-induced vomit. He then lay next to the puddle and emitted loud, groaning noises. There was no immediate effect, but after several minutes of moaning, the patients began to wake up and complain.

Before long, a guard was seen walking down the hall to investigate the matter. He looked in Vengence's cell and saw the large patient glaring back with a small puddle of vomit next to him.

"Stay away, Terran," he said to the guard. "I do not need your assistance."

The guard spoke some lingo into his radio and waited. A few more minutes passed before backup arrived and opened Vengence's cell door.

"C26, let's at least take you to medical where you can get examined," an officer suggested.

Vengence rose to his feet, feigning illness. "I will allow you to take me to medical," he agreed. "but only because it is in the best interest of my immediate survival."

"That's perfectly fine, let's just get you there."

Vengence was escorted by the guards to a golf cart and driven to a building on the other side of the courtyard. The guards were swapped and the medical building security assisted Vengence in entering. He was shown to an examination room where a doctor and orderly waited to help him.

"Stomach problems, eh?" the doctor asked.

"Negative," Vengence replied as he stood up.

"Then what seems to be the problem?"

"My problem is being imprisoned by Terran scum!"

Before the nearby guard could grab his radio, Vengence grabbed him and flipped him onto the examination table, face up. The orderly tried to grab him from behind, but Vengence swung his arm back and clobbered him in the side of the head. As the orderly recoiled, he then delivered a chop to the security guard's throat.

The security guard hacked and gasped for air as Vengence grabbed his radio and smashed it. He then snatched the incapacitated guard's stun baton and ran past the cowering doctor out of the building. Stepping outside, Vengence made a beeline for the security building.

He dashed over to the covered walkway and stopped at the door. Extracting the key card he received from Stupor, he eagerly swiped it in the scanner. A red light blinked briefly, but little else happened. He swiped it a few more times, but to no avail. The door remained locked.

It appears my earlier presumption was correct, he thought to himself with a frown. *The scanners are reset and I will have to find another way in.*

Vengence quickly returned to the courtyard and noticed dim light coming from Lanzendorf's office. On the other side of the large bay window he could see Lanzendorf sitting at his computer, typing on the keyboard.

It is the only way, Vengence thought to himself and approached the window. He reared back the stun baton and threw it at the bay window. The glass shattered with an earsplitting crash, causing Lanzendorf to fall out of his chair in surprise. He stood up just in time to see Vengence jumping in after the baton and staring down at him.

"What the hell?!" he exclaimed.

Lanzendorf moved to run around him, but he was quickly grabbed by his shirt. Vengence then delivered a harsh slap to Lanzendorf's face, the force causing him to spin wildly and fall to a prone position. Lanzendorf propped himself up with his arm and wiped saliva from his mouth, eyes wide. Just as he looked up at Vengence, he was yanked off his feet and hurled out the bay window, landing in the wet grass in a crumpled heap.

"Lay in the dirt where you belong, you filth," Vengence snapped, and ran out the office door.

He immediately recognized the hallway from when he was first checked in and ran through the reception's back room to the patient storage room. On entering the room, a massive horde of orderlies and security guards stormed after him, stun batons and syringes at the ready. Vengence was immediately engulfed by the crowd, sedated, and restrained.

"I will escape from this damned place if it is the last thing I ever do, you bastards!" Vengence shouted drunkenly as he was dragged toward an empty isolation chamber. “I will not tolerate such dishonor!”

Chapter Eight

The next morning, Lanzendorf found himself personally called to Mr. Bark's office.

"Mr. Lanzendorf, there are a couple things I wanted to go over regarding last night's activity," he mentioned. "I just need a bit of clarity."

"Of course, sir," Lanzendorf agreed, standing just as straight as always.

"According to your incident report, you were sitting at your computer when suddenly it made a tremendous buzzing noise."

"Yes, that's correct, sir."

"And the sound startled you and you fell out of your chair and through the bay window?"

"That is absolutely correct, sir."

"That bay window is quite large."

"It is large and thin. Might I also add that my chair hit it first, giving my body a better means to shatter it."

"You also have a mark on your face that you never mentioned in your incident report."

"Oh?" Lanzendorf rubbed a large bruise that had appeared on his cheek and feigned surprise, his eyes wide. "So I see. I must have gotten this when I landed in the grass."

"You fell backward out the window and then landed on your face in the grass?"

"With all due respect, sir, do you believe I'm lying to you?"

"I don't believe you're lying, but I'm sure you can understand me when I say that this incident report seems very weird and difficult to follow."

"I'm not sure what you expect me to say," Lanzendorf replied, giving him a critical look. "I mean, I suppose I could make it more believable, but I personally prefer to stick right to the facts on paperwork. My method of writing incident reports has never done me any wrong in the five years I've spent running security in this facility."

"I have no doubts about your ability to write a shift report, Mr. Lanzendorf, but you have to understand that it doesn't make sense. It may very well simply be in the way you're explaining it."

"Sir, I am embarrassed that this happened. I am William Lanzendorf, and I accidentally broke my window because I was spooked by a sound coming out of a computer. How does it affect my image when people know that stupid things like that happen to the facility's security manager? I have a reputation to maintain!"

Mr. Bark pulled off his eyeglasses and rubbed the bridge of his nose. "So many strange things have been happening over the course of only one week," he complained. "Especially ever since C26 showed up."

"I understand," Lanzendorf empathized. "But at least we are making steady progress with him, however slow. I've been closely working with Dr. Perez on a medication plan that will keep him much more compliant with our procedures."

"Is it really that necessary?"

"High security standards, my friend. This is a

perfect facility and I will accept nothing less than perfection from my department. These strange incidents end today."

"If you say so, Mr. Lanzendorf. And for the sake of this facility, I hope you are right. If you don't mind using your laptop for today, I'll have an engineer check out your machine."

Lanzendorf nodded and left Mr. Bark's office with an insidious smirk. As he stepped into the elevator, he passed Mr. Jenkins.

"What's up, Bill? Looks like you got punched right in the face," he observed, holding the door opened.

"Screw you too," Lanzendorf replied with a flat look. "By the way, I wanted to thank you for your support on C26 sticking around, as agreed."

As Mr. Jenkins reached to shake his hand, he felt a wad of money hiding on his palm. "Like I always say, it pays to scratch each other's backs," Mr. Jenkins chuckled. "But I'm telling you, I still don't know how the hell he got voted to stay."

"Politics can be strange, but it helps to have the chips in your favor," Lanzendorf replied with a smirk. "I'll see you later, I have some business to catch up on."

Mr. Jenkins sportily pointed at him as the elevator doors closed.

***

As Vengence entered the common room, he was greeted by an approaching Stupor.

"Dear friend Vengence, hello!" he welcomed with an excessively proper tone. "I shall not hug you for fear of you beating me up! But I shall, however, wish you a dandy how-dee-doo!"

As soon as Stupor finished his silly greeting, Vengence apathetically walked past him and sat down a table. Patients, as if on cue, began to drift away from him.

Stupor turned to say something to him, but was interrupted by Lanzendorf bumping him out of the way with his shoulder.

"Get out of my way, rodent," he muttered in passing.

Stupor watched as Lanzendorf walked across the room and laid his briefcase on a table not far from Vengence. He then left it to get some food from tray pick-up. On returning to his chair, he opened the briefcase to reveal his work laptop. He extracted the device and took a few bites of his Mexican pizza while waiting for it to boot up. Taking a large bite as he logged in, Lanzendorf managed to dribble some cheese down onto his chin.

He stood up and moved quickly toward tray pick-up once more to retrieve a napkin. Stupor, seizing the great opportunity, wandered over to his laptop and discretely pressed a few buttons. He then scampered back to Vengence's table and twiddled his thumbs.

"Mr. Lanzendorf looks like he stood in front of a tractor-trailer," Stupor said to him. "What do you think happened?"

"That is precisely what happened," Vengence muttered sarcastically.

Lanzendorf returned to his table and on sight of his laptop, dropped his jaw, gawking. He gave his laptop a baffled stare for a few moments before looking about the room with a scowl. He noticed Vengence watching him, unafraid.

"Did you do this to my computer?" he asked sharply, answered only by Vengence's quiet stare. "Did you hear me, baldy? I'm asking if you're the one who turned my damn laptop screen upside-down!"

"Your screen has been turned upside-down?" Vengence asked, cracking a mild smile. "I do not know how to do that, but I find your frustration amusing. How is your face, by the way?"

Lanzendorf glowered at Vengence and puffed his chest out. "The only reason you're still here is because of me," he bragged. "You'll soon realize exactly how horrible that is, you mammoth. Just wait, because later today you won't even be able to stand properly. Would you like to know why? Because I'm going to drug you so much it makes your eyes spin."

"Stop butchering the English language with those contractions," Vengence commanded him. "Take some your misplaced pride and apply it to your words."

Lanzendorf moved closer to Vengence's face and with venom lacing every word, hissed, "Why don'cha do sumpin about it."

Anger coursing through his body, Vengence

reared his fist back, ready to strike. Before he had a chance to swing, Stupor's shrill voice pierced the room.

"Boy howdy!" he cried as he slammed his face on his table, piercing the room with a loud crack.

Everyone in the room stopped and stared at him. He looked up at Lanzendorf and Vengence and gave a cheerful swing of his arm.

"That took care of the ornery little varmint!" he exclaimed in a southern dialect.

Lanzendorf distractedly rolled his eyes and returned to his table, putting his laptop away and eating his food with a frown.

Stupor stared forward, drumming his fingers on the table lightly. "So Vengence," he began. "What exactly did Lanzendorf mean by drugging you up?"

Without answering his question, Vengence stood up and walked over to the common room's collection of board games. Stupor watched in curiosity as Vengence searched through them. Tapping his index finger on a box, he extracted it and returned to Stupor.

"Hey Vengence, you should be proud of me!" Stupor asked. "I haven't used any contractions all morn—oops! I am sorry!"

"I am not concerned with your disregard for your language right now," he responded with a neutral expression. "Are you able to play chess?"

"Kinda!" Stupor's response returned a critical look. He pointed back and eagerly insisted, "That was not a contraction."

Vengence frowned slightly and opened the box, placing all the pieces inside the top prior to unfolding the game board.

"I want to play a game of chess with you," he said to Stupor without looking at him.

"You want to play a game with me?" Stupor asked, confused and mildly suspicious. "Why?"

"Why not?" Vengence asked back, raising an eyebrow.

Stupor cocked his head to the side for a few moments, then shrugged his shoulders prior to setting up the pieces on his nearest half of the board. He periodically paused his task to swing his arm happily.

"This is gonna be so awesome!" he spouted. "Am I white or black?"

"I do not care," Vengence uttered.

"I suppose I'll go first, then!"

The two men played for a few minutes and appeared to be evenly matched. As Stupor made his moves, Vengence watched his mannerisms closely as he calculated different possibilities. He clearly saw see Stupor taking the game seriously, subtly pointing at places on the board while imagining consequences for his available actions. Stupor took notably longer than Vengence to end his turn, but his strategy was consequently unpredictable.

"You're really good!" Stupor complimented.

"Likewise," he replied, stroking his chin. "So why are you actually stuck here?"

"Meh, I don't even know anymore. I'd say it's

a conspiracy if I were anyone special, but I'm just another crazy guy to them! They say I attacked a magistrate during my trial, but I really wasn't in the courtroom! Nobody believes me, though."

It seems he is more open to sharing legitimate information if he is distracted by something gratifying, Vengence thought to himself. "If you were not in the courtroom, then where were you?"

"I don't really like to talk about that," Stupor said, shaking his head. "I lose potential friends that way."

"What if I told you that I came to this time from roughly one thousand years in the future?" Vengence asked.

Stupor stopped and looked at Vengence for a moment. "Really?" he asked.

"Affirmative."

"Didn't know that," Stupor chuckled and looked back at the board.

"Of course you do not believe me," Vengence grumbled.

"More like it's a hard thing to believe!"

"It is just as difficult to believe as your name being Baron Von Stupor."

Stupor smiled under his mask and replied, "I guess that's just part of my charm!"

Vengence stopped conversing for a moment to contemplate his next move.

"So since we're being all open about stuff..." Stupor said, leaning close to Vengence. "Promise you won't tell anybody, but when I was in the courtroom, I think I might have gotten sucked into another dimension temporarily."

"Another... dimension?" Vengence asked, his eyebrows raised.

"Yeah! It wasn't a friendly dimension, either. I don't know how to explain it, but it all started during my trial. I was listening to a bunch of lies and next thing you know I was in another world!

"When I opened my eyes, I was in a cave full of monsters and I was standing on some kind of ornate pedestal. There was a really pretty girl there that I used to know, too! She was scared and called my name for help. When I saw her, I jumped off of my pedestal and boldly began to fight the monsters. There were a lot though, so I sort of gunned for the leader. Cut the snake at the head, you know? Thankfully they were sorta humanoid, so I was pretty competent in how to handle them. I blacked out before I could save her, though. When I woke up, I was back in jail."

Vengence looked back at Stupor, stupefied.

"I know it's pretty hard to believe," Stupor continued. "That's why I try not to talk about it much. I don't know if that girl was ever rescued or not. I hope she was, though. She wasn't the nicest person, but she definitely didn't deserve to be dinner like that. She was the closest I had to a real life friend from those days.

"The strange thing is that those monsters all looked at me like I was crazy when I tried to save that girl. It makes me suspect that I was actually switched with an evil copy of myself, to keep the multiverse balanced. I also think that the evil me is why everyone thinks I attacked the magistrate.

"So the end result was that I went to another world, tried to save my friend, returned to Earth, and eventually got framed for crimes that I didn't really commit."

Vengence shook his head in disgust.

"You are clueless to how insane you actually are for having delusions like those," he said to Stupor coldly, and stood up. "You do not deserve to leave this place any more than that idiotic fighter pilot does."

Vengence walked away as Stupor slouched in his chair, morbidly offended. As the words sank in, Stupor became irate and stood up quickly. He furiously slapped his chair, causing it to clatter away.

"You listen here, Vengence!" he demanded, marching directly over to the giant.

Vengence turned to face him, surprised and curious at Stupor's outburst. Facing Stupor, he was met with an angry finger jabbing him right in the chest.

"I do know what my story implies about me! I know it sounds crazy! I'm not a stupid kid!" he spat. "But just because I believe that's the truth and just because there's no proof to substantiate it doesn't mean it couldn't have happened, Mr. Time Traveler!"

"I offered you that information about me and you also chose not to believe," Vengence argued. "Your argument is null and void."

"I said it's hard to believe, not that I didn't

believe it! I'm giving you the benefit of the doubt here because I'm your friend, even if you don't wanna be mine."

Vengence stared into the vacant, soulless eyes of Stupor's mask, unable to read his face. He was thoroughly surprised by Stupor's explosive tirade, yet made no attempt to show it.

"Very well," he resigned after a brief moment of silence. "I will offer you benefit of the doubt for now... But only because every time you show yourself as nothing more than a typical ignorant Terran, you wash away that notion with a subtle act of intelligence that I find intriguing."

Stupor and Vengence then noticed that every person in the room was watching the pair in a flabbergasted, deafening silence. Vengence made his way past Stupor and uncomfortably returned to the table. Stupor closely followed, grumpily setting his chair back up and sitting in it.

Vengence examined the game board and contemplated his next move. After pondering for a few moments, he captured another of Stupor's pieces and gestured for him to continue.

"I'm a good arguer," Stupor muttered as he observed the board.

A few more turns went by in complete silence as Vengence worked up Stupor's concentration further.

After capturing another of Stupor's pieces, Vengence casually asked, "Why does Lanzendorf have such a grudge against you?"

"Mr. Lanzendorf's an interesting guy," Stupor

replied. "One thing I've noticed is that he's a lot like a spoiled kid. If he doesn't get the attention he wants, he causes trouble."

"What does that have to do with you?"

"He runs his ship on fear and fear alone. The fact that I'm the only one he can't crack bothers him more than anything else. It makes breaking my spirit a life mission for him or something."

"He seems to posses a lot of political power," Vengence continued as he watched his piece get captured. "Why bother resisting someone if it would only serve to make you miserable?"

Stupor looked toward Vengence and coldly stated, "I don't like bullies."

"You do not like bullies. That is all?"

"Pretty much. I put my foot down with them a long time ago."

On making that comment, Stupor moved a knight and cheerfully declared checkmate.

"You seem to be much more intelligent than you lead anyone to believe, Baron Von Stupor," Vengence complimented, sitting back in his chair and crossing his arms.

Stupor bolted upright in his chair and looked off to the side. "The knight's movements strongly suggest that he teleports around during battle," he mused. "Teleporters weren't invented by then, though, were they?"

Vengence, uninterested in his musing, stared at Stupor and replied, "Congratulations on your victory." He then stood up and walked away to another nearby table, staring out the window.

Chapter Nine

"Patient C26!" Lanzendorf called sharply.

The abruptness of the noise caused Stupor to snort awake. Looking around, he saw Vengence still sitting at the other table, his head propped up by his hand. He apathetically glanced over his shoulder at Lanzendorf.

"We're going to send you on a trip to La-La Land, you big behemoth," Lanzendorf chuckled.

This isn't good, Stupor thought to himself.

Vengence was sternly escorted by Lanzendorf, Abernathy, and an older security guard named Wilson outside the common room.

Stupor casually got up and wandered in their direction while trying to remain inconspicuous. He watched them from afar as they traversed the courtyard and entered the medical building via the covered walkway entrance. Stupor quickly entered after them and approached the desk as they went into the back.

"Hi, Stacy! How are you doing this fine day?" he asked the stone-faced receptionist.

"Bored. How are you?" she asked in reply.

"Oh, I'll know here in a few minutes."

Before she could even reply, Stupor stepped through the door into the private area. He could hear Lanzendorf down the hall and followed the sound of his voice with Stacy hot in pursuit, protesting his daring move.

Stupor boldly walked into the room and saw Vengence with his fist balled up, as if about to strike. Vengence, the guards, and Lanzendorf all gave Stupor a slightly surprised glance on his entrance.

"Hey, what's in that?" Stupor asked Wilson, pointing at a filled syringe in Lanzendorf's hand.

"None of your business, B256," Lanzendorf spat. "Get out of here!"

"I wasn't talking to you, buddy!" Stupor said to Lanzendorf with his chest puffed out. "Don't interrupt my conversations, Mr. Big Buttinsky!"

Lanzendorf chuckled at Stupor. "Someone's a little snappy."

Stupor completely ignored Lanzendorf and continued speaking to Abernathy. "What's Mr. Lanzendorf going to do?"

"It's none of your business," the guard nastily answered. "Get out!"

"Are you listening to me?" Lanzendorf asked, growing irritated.

Vengence observed the conversation, curious.

"Hey, Officer Abernathy," Stupor continued. "is Mr. Lanzendorf even licensed for this kind of thing? I think he's taking things a little too far."

"Shut up, Abernathy!" Lanzendorf shot just as the guard opened his mouth. Lanzendorf then moved to Stupor, vainly attempting to shove him out. Stupor effortlessly wormed around his arms and moved right back to Abernathy.

"Sorry, I didn't expect this guy who looks like he got hit by a car to be all rude up in this joint," Stupor apologized. "So what was it you were going to say—"

The very end of Stupor's sentence was cut off by Lanzendorf, who by then grabbed Stupor by his shoulders and threw him across the room. Stupor stumbled over himself and crashed into a cabinet. While he was disoriented, Lanzendorf kicked his feet out from under his body. Stupor awkwardly fell to the floor, propped up by the cabinet door. Lanzendorf then bent down and grabbed Stupor by his hair, putting his face close to his.

"Do you see that I'm talking to you now?!" he shrieked. "I'm talking to you, so now you answer to me! Not Wilson, not Abernathy! You answer to me!"

Stupor glanced up at Vengence, who merely observed from the examination bed. Abernathy and Wilson gave awkward glances to each other, unsure how to handle the situation.

"Say Vengence," Stupor said, lightly tugging on Lanzendorf's arm to get a better view of him. "Do you think you could ask the guard if–"

Stupor had no time to finish his sentence as Lanzendorf screamed in a murderous rage and used all of his might to slam Stupor's head into the cabinet door. "Abernathy, Wilson! Get him the hell out of here!" Lanzendorf shouted as he angrily wiped some saliva from his mouth.

He looked at the doorway and saw an agape Stacy standing with her hand over her mouth in complete horror. "If you tell anyone, you're dead. Dead!" he threatened.

Both Abernathy and Wilson uncomfortably

assisted Stupor out of the examination room and into the waiting area. Wilson bore a disturbed expression on his face.

"Now," he said to Vengence, picking up the syringe. "We can finally get back to your—"

The moment Lanzendorf faced Vengence, he received a crushing punch in the nose. He heard an audible pop as his bone was shattered. Blood exploded from the cavity as his instantaneously unconscious body bounced off the cabinet and crumpled to the floor in a heap. Vengence then calmly walked to the waiting room and observed Stupor swaying slightly. Abernathy and Wilson ran past Vengence in the other direction, alerted by the sound of Lanzendorf's limp body hitting the floor. Vengence chose to follow Stupor as he wobbled out the waiting room door and sat on a nearby bench, holding his head.

"Why do you so stubbornly insist on helping me?" he asked as Stupor checked his head for any signs of blood. "I do not understand your utter fascination with helping me escape."

"That's just what friends do for each other—"

"How many times must I remind you that I am not your friend? Furthermore, why are you so interested in helping me despite my eternal disassociation with the idea of being your friend? It is so selfless an act that it is suspicious."

"You're so different from the other patients," Stupor said. "The others all have their problems, but if you look at the big picture you don't seem to be sick at all."

Vengence gave Stupor a skeptical frown and crossed his arms.

"Look, neither one of us feels like we belong here," Stupor said wistfully. "I believe you when you say it!" Stupor then looked off toward the courtyard. "They tell me that I'll get out when I'm all better, but I feel perfectly fine... like I can't get any better if I tried," he lamented. "If neither one of us belongs here, then at least I can make one of our dreams come true." Looking back to Vengence, he added, "And believe me, with the way you act you'll need every ounce of help you can get."

Vengence narrowed his eyes at Stupor.

"I'm serious!" Stupor asserted. "You might be a super brute, but that only helps in fights! Until you start strategizing and manipulating people, you're never gonna get out of here, ever. So I'll manipulate people for you, to help you escape!"

"Speaking of your manipulation," Vengence wondered. "is there some kind of ulterior motive for not fighting Lanzendorf? I know you are more capable than the pathetic show you put on in there."

"What do you think the asylum would do if I fought back? Besides, there's a security camera in that room plus one witness. If I can get anyone to start asking questions, Mr. Lanzendorf will assuredly receive a nasty visit from the board in due time."

"I believe I may have already taken care of that," Vengence chuckled, mildly impressed.

***

"Sir, I only need a chance to explain myself," Lanzendorf insisted. His voice now had a distinct nasal twang due to the blood-soaked toilet paper clots plugged in his nostrils.

"A chance to explain yourself?" a furious Dr. Bark exclaimed. "I think the security feed does a pretty good job of explaining what happened in there!"

"You didn't hear what B256 was even saying, sir! He was antagonizing me! You can't make out what he was saying because of that stupid mask of his. I told you we should have him remove it."

Mr. Bark angrily rewound the footage on the computer again, aggressively jabbing his finger at the monitor.

"What about this, where you slammed that young man's head into the cabinet, hm? Was he antagonizing you at that moment as well?!" he interrogated.

"His words. They weakened me, sir. I briefly lost myself and cannot apologize enough..."

"And then you removed the guards from the room with a known dangerous patient. Did you honestly think you could take him on by yourself with your 'high security standards'? It seems like you paid a high price for that misjudgment!"

"But sir—"

"Did you plan to file an incident report? Hm? Or did you forget? It's only been two hours."

"I… I forgot to write the incident report, yes! Sir, I'm still feeling light-headed from the attack, and very stressed."

"You are not even qualified to be providing medication for patients! You are supposed to be the security manager of this facility. You are not a doctor and you are not a nurse! What you were doing is illegal! Does Dr. Perez know about this? You can rest assured I will be going straight to her once I'm done talking to you!

"I also hear you physically threatened Stacy Wilson in medical as well. You have overstepped your bounds before, but to my knowledge never to this extent such as this. Your behavior is abhorrent and ghastly, Mr. Lanzendorf, and if it weren't for your blackened eyes and bleeding nose I'd have never noticed a thing."

Lanzendorf simply stood in silence, his hands behind his back. His face was firm but in his eyes seeded doubt, a feeling he hadn't known in years.

"Frankly, I am terrified to know exactly how many patients you've done things like this to," Mr. Bark continued. "I'm afraid that if I knew, our facility would be shut down instantaneously!

"I admire your talents and our reviews under your watch have been the best we've ever seen, but I can't let this go."

"S-sir, no! You can't!" Lanzendorf pleaded, by now sweating bullets.

"Yes I can, and I will. It pains me to say this, Mr. Lanzendorf, but I'm going to suspend your position here indefinitely."

"What?!"

"Your absence will keep you from shattering your credibility any more than you already have. You are not permitted to return to the premises until the board meeting next Friday. During this time, your performance will be under very strict review. We will also be investigating some more feeds for instances of possible patient abuse."

"This is completely unnecessary, sir! I insist that I be allowed to continue my work!"

"Mr. Lanzendorf, your actions could get you prosecuted and you're upset about not being able to work? Get out of my office and go home!"

Lanzendorf looked into the director's angry eyes for a few furious moments before registering his command. Slowly, he turned and left with a look of seething hatred on his face.

"We'll see what the board says about this..." he muttered under his breath.

***

Stupor and Vengence were calmly sitting in the common room when in stormed Lanzendorf. He darted his attention in all directions and located the two in seconds. He stamped over to them and shot the two a horrid look, breathing heavily through clenched teeth.

"Holy crap! What happened to you?" Stupor asked with a laugh. Vengence stared grumpily.

Lanzendorf placed his palms on the table and glared at the two with murderous loathing.

"I know you two planned this..." he muttered with venom lacing every word.

Vengence and Stupor returned blank stares.

"Don't act stupid!" he spat, struggling not to fire toilet paper clots out of his nose with every consonant. "I know you two did this to me. You two planned to get me suspended! That was it, all along! Well, when I come back I will take care of you both once and for all. *Once... and... for... all!*"

A moment passed and a stifled laugh escaped Stupor. Lanzendorf glared at him with such fury that his forehead vein seemed like it would pop at any moment.

"I'm really sorry, Mr. La–pbthbth..." Stupor struggled, unable to complete a sentence. "Your voice sounds really funny..."

Lanzendorf leered at Vengence, who by then was also fighting a light smile. Drawing in a deep breath, he furiously stomped away while flailing his arms angrily and ranting incoherently.

"Wow! He did a really mad thing!" Beeboo exclaimed from behind Stupor, loudly clapping his hands on his cheeks in surprise. "Lanzendorf he gone?"

"Yep, but probably only for a little while." Stupor responded.

Beeboo proudly thrust his fists into the air and exclaimed, "Hooray! Lanzendorf he gone for little while!"

Beeboo danced for a moment, then quickly lost interest. Sitting down, he began eyeballing the checkers game box on the shelves lovingly.

"So Vengence!" Stupor called, upbeat. "With Lanzendorf gone, you might be able to escape."

Vengence looked gave Stupor an inquisitive look, stroking his chin. "Affirmative... this would be the most opportune time for an escape," he agreed. "Baron Von Stupor, I have been thinking about the things you have said over the time that I have known you. After much consideration, I have decided to extend a proposition to you."

"You're going to propose to me, Vengence?" Stupor asked with a chuckle.

"Technically, yes," Vengence responded, his brows furrowed. "However, I already regret it."

"Oh, don't be such a poop. What's up?"

"Against my better judgment, I have reason to believe that we may be able to help each other out as a team."

Stupor leaned on the table by his elbow and gave Vengence a skeptical look. "If you escape, they're not going to let you smuggle ice cream cake in for me, man." he scoffed.

"Stupor, if you believe you do not belong here, then why not escape with me and eat all of the ice cream cake that you want?"

Stupor's eyes widened with surprise. "You... you really want me to come with you? For real?" he asked, unsure of what to think.

"Despite every attempt I make to drive you away, you obstinately refuse to stop helping me," Vengence explained. "You are enigmatic, socially awkward, and a blabbering fool, but you hide an intelligence that I do not see in many people.

"I am in some perverse way convinced that you have a method to your madness. Ergo, I feel that if we can work together, we both might be able to escape this dump."

Stupor drummed his fingers in nervousness. He was wholly unfamiliar with the prospect of working on a legitimate team with someone. He was both excited at the dream of freedom, yet fearful of it as well.

"If I go with you, the authorities will come after us, though..." he debated.

"Whether you come with me or stay is your choice," Vengence reminded him. "However, I will capitalize on this opportunity and if I escape, I will not come back for you. You will wind up right where you were before I arrived."

Stupor fidgeted in his chair. *I have the chance to change things...* he thought to himself. *I have the chance to choose my own future. I'm scared of it.* He then lamented aloud, "I know they're not gonna let me out, because I'm never going to get any better than I am right now..."

Stupor gestured to Vengence to wait while he turned away to think. He stared forlornly out the window and watched inmates playing basketball as he thought.

I would be able to choose my own path in life. I wouldn't be held down by everyone's differing beliefs. I also certainly wouldn't be victimized anymore by Mr. Lanzendorf.

But if I leave, the rest of my life will be running from authorities. I would also be leaving behind Jörg, my first actual friend here. I also can't handle myself like Vengence can, surviving and fighting and stuff.

"Vengence," Stupor answered, a solemn tone in his voice. "I would love to escape the asylum with you and breathe the air of freedom again. But Jörg is my only other friend here. If I escape, I'd be leaving the asylum on principle alone. If I leave Jörg behind, I feel like I'd be going back on the very principles I try to uphold."

"Whatever," Vengence replied. "I do not care about your reasons."

"I still want to help you escape, though. I just think it's better for me if I stayed here. Your offer means a lot to me, though."

"Stupor, you are correct that I cannot escape this place with brute force," Vengence agreed, swiftly changing the subject. "Therefore I need you to tell me everything you know about the facility's infrastructure."

***

Lanzendorf had everyone gathered inside the security building break room for an emergency meeting. As he spoke, he typed furiously on his laptop.

"I'm writing a passdown form for everyone that isn't on duty," Lanzendorf informed them. "No one will have an excuse for being unaware of what I have to say. Every single guard in this facility had better sign it."

Lanzendorf could barely ignore the guards'

snickering due to his toilet paper clot-induced speech impediment.

"In light of the recent escape attempts, I want absolutely everyone to have key cards reissued and every lock reset on a shift-by-shift basis," he continued. "From now on, individual guards will post exclusively to each building. Their key cards will only grant access to the building they are posted at and any other area that is communal to all employees. Every guard must be buzzed in to access the security building.

"I won't be in the office for a few days, so everyone will report to Abernathy for everything and then Abernathy will immediately contact me for explicit instruction."

Lanzendorf's face reddened as the snickering continued. "Every single guard better sign that form and return it to Cheryl!" he declared as his impatience grew. "If you don't, you're as good as fired!"

He angrily glared at the guards, who were visibly unable to keep quiet. Losing his patience, he raised his voice to shout. "Stop laughing and get back to—"

Lanzendorf was unable to finish his sentence as one of the toilet paper wads shot out of his nostril. As he juggled it, his nose began to bleed again and dripped onto his white shirt.

The guards instantly began laughing and left the room. Lanzendorf, after getting the wad back in, grabbed a box of plastic forks in a rage and threw it across the room.

"I hate that goddamn kid!" he screamed.

***

"Hey Jörg," Stupor said, staring at the ceiling from his bunk. "What do you think about me leaving here? Like escaping? Do you think I'd even survive on the run from the law?"

"Nein," the cellmate replied flatly.

"That was blunt," Stupor observed. He bent over the bunk's edge and peered at Jörg. "You feeling okay?"

"Mir geht heute viel durch den Kopf."

"You seem a little upset. I guess we all have our off days!" Stupor then lay back down. "I was just curious, because with every passing month it seems more and more apparent that I won't be going anywhere.

"In the year-ish that I've been here, the only friends I've ever had are you and Vengence. But he is supposed to be leaving soon and then it'll be just us again.

"Life here isn't that bad, though. The room and board is paid for by the government. There's also plenty of people who talk to you, even though it's the kind of conversations adults have when they humor children. I'm hardly accepted here, but it's the closest I've ever gotten to it."

"Die Welt da draußen ist viel deprimierender als jedes Irrenhaus," Jörg commented. "Dir geht es hier viel besser."

"Mr. Lanzendorf got suspended today, did

you know that?" Stupor asked him.

"Was?" Jörg uttered, surprised. "Wie ist das passiert?"

"Yeah, it surprised me too, but in a way I saw it coming. Let's just say that even the mighty Mr. Lanzendorf has his weaknesses and I capitalized on one!"

Jörg jumped off the bed and looked at Stupor with wide eyes. He seemed mildly worried.

"Dein Leben wird die Hölle, wenn er zurückkommt. Er wird dich niemals in Ruhe lassen!"

"Are you really worried, Jörg?"

"Ja," Jörg replied, broadly nodding his head. "Du wirst für den Rest deines Lebens isoliert sein, wenn er zurückkommt."

"I'm not worried about the consequences to be honest," Stupor chuckled lightly. "I think it was for the greater good, and the other inmates seem to have a brighter glow of hope.

"Even long after Mr. Lanzendorf comes back, everyone will know that he's not as omnipotent as he wants everyone to think he is. Hopefully everybody will finally learn that the evil god of the asylum bleeds the same blood we do."

"Du hast solch eine interessante Seele," Jörg told him with a greatly intrigued smile. "Sie ist so dunkel, aber dennoch unbefleckt. Ich hoffe, sie wird eines Tages Teil meiner Sammlung."

"Good night, buddy. Tomorrow is the start of an overdue vacation in the absence of Big Bad Lanzendorf."

***

"Staying in the asylum is the best choice. It makes everything so much easier to accomplish. Kill or be killed. Choose or be chosen. Make a choice or a choice will be made for you. The ball's in my court now! Do something about it!"

Chapter Ten

"Sleeping gets on my nerves at times," Stupor said, wiping at his eyes under his mask. "Hey Jörg, do you ever have those dreams where you wake up multiple times before actually waking up? I kept having dreams where I would wake up and you'd be on the bed ladder, smiling at me. It happened about four times before I woke up for real!"

Stupor climbed down to the ground level to see that Jörg was not even present in the room. "Huh," he muttered to himself, feeling silly.

He proceeded out of the living quarters and across the courtyard to the commons. Stepping inside, he noticed Ralph sitting at the nearest table.

"You'd be surprised how few words rhyme with your name, man!" he said, not even entirely sure if Ralph was hearing him. "All I know is 'mouth', and that's more of an off-rhyme than anything."

"Yup," Ralph replied, staring forward. His eyelids fluttered slightly.

"What are you doing here if Mr. Lanzendorf is suspended, anyway?"

"He might want coffee..."

"What if he doesn't need coffee?"

Ralph looked at Stupor with glazed eyes. He furrowed his monobrow lightly and looked down toward the floor.

"I'm tired," he uttered, his mouth parted ever

slightly.

"Would you mind doing me a favor?"

Ralph slowly stood up and faced Stupor. His shoulders remained slouched. "Yeah, I'll do it."

"If you could figure out how Lanzendorf has the security department organized, that would be pretty useful."

Ralph stared at Stupor. He narrowed his eyes as if in deep thought. As the two stared at each other, it was as if time ground to a halt.

"Wait a minute..." Ralph said. "You're not supposed to know that, right?"

"Nope!"

Ralph paused as his brain processed Stupor's unexpectedly straightforward answer. He looked back at Stupor, a lost expression on his face.

"Why do you want it?"

"How can I follow Mr. Lanzendorf's plan if I don't know what it is?" Stupor asked matter-of-factly with his hands on his hips.

"Oh. Well, I guess that's okay."

"While you're at it, could you make me some coffee, too? Six sugars, six creamers."

"Yeah, I'll do it."

"You're the coffee champion!"

Stupor watched Ralph perform a half-hearted waddle, uttering "blub, blub, blub" at awkward intervals.

"That's my boy," Stupor chuckled to himself and scanned the room for Vengence.

Seeing him at the far end of one of the long tables, Stupor began moving toward him.

"I don't think so, B256," Abernathy spoke, grabbing his shoulder from behind. "You're not allowed to talk to him anymore."

"Why not?" Stupor asked, slightly confused.

"You're not gonna talk to him because he's violent, you're smart, and you're both crazy. Go somewhere else."

"That's an awfully mean thing to say," Stupor commented. "Is everything alright?"

"I'm in charge while Mr. Lanzendorf is away. If I see you go within five yards of C26, you're immediately headed to solitary."

"How many tiles is that? I'd like a visual aid so I don't accidentally go under the limit."

"B256, go sit somewhere and behave."

Stupor obediently sat at a table as close to five yards to Vengence as humanly possible. He then interlaced his fingers and began to look around. He noticed Vengence carefully staring at Abernathy, who bore a suspicious look on his face.

Stupor, receiving an inspiration, stood up and fetched paper and a pencil from a game box. He then wrote a message on the paper and crumpled it up.

Vengence looked onward in curiousity as Stupor tossed the paper to him. The paper barely missed the table, shooting between the surface and attached bench and ultimately coming to a rest at his feet. He leaned down and picked it up, beginning to uncrumple it.

Before he could read it, Abernathy snatched

it out of his hand.

"Do you honestly think I didn't see any of that?" he scolded as Vengence glared, unafraid. "You two are to going stay five yards away from each other or I'm putting him in solitary, got it? And stop passing notes, notes are not allowed!"

Abernathy uncrumpled the note and silently read to himself:

Say Vengence, do you think Officer Abernathy ever noticed that big ol' booger near his lower lip? How does it even get there? I bet he eats them!
-B.V.S.

Abernathy quickly wiped at his mouth and examined his hand. Seeing nothing, his surprise turned to frustration. "Alright, that does it!" he shouted impatiently. "B256, it's solitary for you!"

Stupor skipped over to Abernathy where he was roughly put in restraints and escorted past several confused guards out of the building.

***

"Quick question: So why can't I talk to Vengence now if I could before Mr. Lanzendorf disappeared?" Stupor asked Abernathy as he was ushered toward his isolation chamber. "Ahh, I bet that has something to do with it."

After Abernathy removed Stupor's restraints, he gave him a rough single-handed shove. Stupor stumbled all the way into the cell and turned to face Abernathy, unfazed.

"As often as you and Mr. Lanzendorf do that to me, I gotta say I'm glad there are no steps on the way in here," he commented.

"I know that you're trying to ruin the security department," Abernathy told him, shooting a dirty look. "You're trying to pick it apart from the inside out. You're really smart if you're able to get Mr. Lanzendorf in so much trouble, but you're not going to pull the wool over my eyes. By the time Mr. Lanzendorf returns, your ace in the hole is going to be transferred to another facility."

"Well, you oughtta make sure the rest of the deck gets transferred, then!"

"What's that supposed to mean?" he asked, giving Stupor a look of mild confusion.

Stupor scratched his chin in thought and said, "I don't actually know... In retrospect it probably doesn't make much sense; I was just trying to think of something quick and witty to say."

Abernathy sneered at Stupor before shutting the chamber door. As Stupor sat down on his bed, he heard conversation outside the chamber.

"Sir, I need to sign the passdown form from Mr. Lanzendorf," a guard said.

"Cheryl has it," he replied bluntly prior to walking back past Stupor's chamber door and out of the building.

"Excuse me," Stupor said aloud to the guard. "May I see the passdown form, too?"

The guard ignored Stupor as he left for the

admin hallway.

***

"Hey buddy," Beeboo said to Vengence with a smirk. "Beeboo hear you want play checker."

"Go away," Vengence told him, observing the common room.

He noticed Abernathy talking to a security guard. Terry, sitting nearby, was looking between Vengence and Abernathy and becoming visibly upset.

"You lie? You still no play checker Beeboo?" Beeboo asked, looking sad.

Vengence turned and snarled in Beeboo's face. Beeboo immediately looked with frightened eyes and exhaled sharply through his nose. Snot spurted out, lightly peppering Vengence's arm. Vengence yanked it back and glowered at Beeboo in disgust.

"You make Beeboo sad!" he declared.

"I will make Beeboo *dead* if he does not leave me alone!" Vengence snapped back, wiping his arm on his pants.

"Other Beeboo?! Beeboo make other Beeboo pay for being beebee... buh... for then be Beeboo Beeboo Beeboo!"

He rose and stomped away angrily. Vengence watched the scrawny man pace around the room until his eyes landed on Terry, who was quickly approaching.

"Just who do you think you are?!" he asked

nastily. "Do you think you're superior to me just because you're so big? I'll have you know I can kick your ass anytime I want to, big guy!"

Vengence opened his mouth to reply, then noticed Abernathy watching him with prying eyes. Vengence looked back down at Terry, then back to Abernathy.

Cowardly bastard, he thought to himself. *That boy is deliberately trying my patience by manipulating the inmates.*

Vengence then felt a small thump against his leg. Looking downward, he caught Terry pulling his foot back from kicking him.

"What are your feelings about the security force here, puny Terran?" Vengence asked him.

"They ain't gonna save you from me, that's what I think!" Terry said, and kicked his leg once more with absolutely no effect.

"How many bones do you think would break if I punched you in your tiny face?" Vengence asked, holding a balled up fist next to Terry's head.

Terry looked at it with his eyes widened once he realized that it was as big as his face. "You know what? You're lucky I'm in a good mood," he said, and turned to walk away.

Vengence reached out and grabbed him by the shoulder, pulling him close.

"Yes," he muttered in Terry's ear. "You are extremely lucky."

Vengence then shoved him hard enough for him to stumble forward a few steps. Terry stared daggers at Vengence while walking away quickly.

"Putting your hands on the inmates? I should put you in solitary for that," Abernathy chided, approaching quickly.

"Feh. You are more than welcome to try, you simpleton," Vengence responded, sitting back in his chair and folding his arms.

Abernathy looked back at the other guards, none of which bothered to follow him. Hearing movement, he looked back at Vengence to see him on his feet with his fist reared back to strike. Abernathy loosed a high scream and scrambled backward, failing to realize that Vengence had never actually swung. After nearly toppling over a chair, he frightfully looked back at a smirking Vengence and realized he had been duped.

"T-that's it! I'm locking you up!" he sputtered angrily as Vengence sat down in his chair.

"Then do it, whelp," Vengence said, folding his arms again.

Abernathy backed further and looked at the other guards, who had been dashing to his aid. They halted once they noticed Abernathy was not in any actual danger and observed from afar. Having an epiphany, Abernathy gave Vengence a critical stare.

"You're just trying to join your friend again, aren't you?" he asked rhetorically. "Well, you can just forget it. You two won't be scheming on my watch."

"Stupor is not my friend, nor am I the only one in this room that has an agenda," Vengence calmly responded.

"What's that supposed to mean?"

Vengence sat back in his chair with a smirk.

"You are pathetic, boy," he emphasized. "At least Lanzendorf can mask his true motives. You, however, are an open book."

Abernathy's mouth opened ever slightly with insult. He jabbed his finger at Vengence, but was unable to say anything.

"I'm gonna... You... You are lucky you don't have any privileges left for me to take away!" he sputtered before storming off.

Even with Lanzendorf out of the picture, we still need to take care of his incompetent stooge, Vengence thought to himself. *Escape is nearly impossible as long as we have his attention.*

***

"We always love the feeling of raindrops on our heads, and yet most of us avoid them as if they were acid. Human beings are the epitome of hypocrisy; it's almost an art form in itself."

***

Stupor jumped awake at the sound of the chamber door opening, unaware he had drifted to sleep.

"Officer Herald! How's it going, buddy?" Stupor asked the guard.

"Come on, B256," he said impatiently.

Stupor tripped over his foot on the way out of the cell and stumbled a bit. Herald caught him as he gripped the door frame.

"I guess I was sleeping kinda hard!" Stupor chuckled.

"You could probably see better if you took that mask off," Herald commented. "How do you even get around?"

"You know, I ask myself the same question," Stupor replied. "I often forget it's even there!"

"No, I mean there are no holes on it except around the mouth. How do you see?"

Stupor leaned in close and said in a low, raspy breath, "Our eyes are one."

Herald backed away and gave Stupor a very uncomfortable gaze.

"Is it lunchtime yet?" Stupor excitedly asked with an energetic swing of his arm.

Herald rolled his eyes and ushered Stupor to the building exit. "Don't get in more trouble," he warned. "Things are way weird enough without Mr. Lanzendorf, so we don't need you stirring up any more crap."

Stupor chuckled as he left for the common room.

***

Vengence sat at a table, clenching his head in his hands as he listened to the ramblings of an inmate named Paul Galliver.

Paul was committed to the asylum against his will after suffering a head trauma and developing a case of paraduplicative amnesia. He dressed in medical scrubs against his will as he was a risk for violent behavior. His brown hair was long and shabby and he sported a full beard, vowing never to cut or shave until his freedom is restored.

"It's the only other form of defiance I have left, you know?" he said to Vengence. "You want to know something really crazy?"

"No," Vengence callously responded, looking up at a smirking Officer Abernathy.

"I might be kept here against my will, but I know for a fact I'm still right here at home," Paul continued. "You see, this whole damn facility is in my basement. They are literally hiding me in my own home; the last place anyone would think to look!"

"I do not care."

"You should! Your rights are being violated! How could you let yourself be broken like this?"

Vengence pursed his lips as a vein began to bulge on his forehead.

"Hey, Vengence!" he heard Stupor call from across the room. "What's shaking?"

Before Stupor could reach him, he was again stopped by Officer Abernathy.

"Stop there, B256! Five yards and no notes!" Abernathy reminded him.

"Oh, okay," Stupor apathetically complied, sitting at a table somewhat near Vengence.

"You know what?" Paul asked Vengence. "I

think that guy in the mask is a mole. He doesn't want anyone to see his face. Personally, I think he's Sean Ritzo in disguise. You know, the IT director? Their squeaky voices sound about the same."

Vengence fought back a chuckle.

"So Vengence, about what's shaking," Stupor called to him from afar. "Are you excited about group therapy on Monday?"

"Stop talking to C26 right now!" Abernathy chided Stupor.

"What's wrong with talking? It's not like I'm writing a note or anything."

"B256, you are not allowed to communicate with C26 in any way, shape, or form! I will lock you up all over again if you don't obey!"

"Why do you keep making up the rules, Mr. Abernathy?" Stupor asked, calmly approaching.

"Because I'm in charge right now and I can get away with it!" Abernathy asserted, jabbing his thumb at himself.

"So you're the new Lanzendorf then, huh?"

"What's that supposed to mean?" Abernathy asked, unsure of whether to be offended or not.

"I guess you could interpret that however you want. What's ironic though, is that a long while back when I was talking to Mr. Lanzendorf, he totally called himself a dependent idiot!"

Abernathy's eyes grew wider and his face bore confusion as he struggled to understand Stupor's statement. After a few moments of thought, he became frustrated and angry.

"Did you say 'ironic'? What's that supposed to mean?!" he asked, raising his voice.

"Idunno. But congratulations on your new position, Mr. Abernathzendorf! Just don't go off slamming patients' heads into cabinets, eh?"

Stupor chuckled lightly and shot Abernathy a thumbs up before sitting back down at his table. Abernathy stood dumbfounded for a moment, struggling to make sense of things.

"Goddamn it!" he swore, growing ever more frustrated.

"You're damn right, Paul," Stupor said to the inmate, distracting his attention from talking to Vengence.

Paul's eyes grew wider as he rose up from his chair. "What do you mean I'm right?" he asked.

"We'll meet later. I'll contact you."

"How do I know I can trust you?"

"I should ask you the same question."

Paul thought to himself for a moment, then nodded his head. He left the table and moved toward the bookshelves. Stupor sat down nearby Vengence and twiddled his thumbs. Abernathy grouchily returned to his post at the entrance, frowning at Stupor.

***

A few boring hours passed in the common room. Stupor continued to sit, his face resting flat on the table. Occasionally, he would look up, surveying the room. Out of the corner of his eye, he noticed Abernathy leaving the room.

Meanwhile, Officer Wilson was punching in for his shift in the security building. As he left the building, Abernathy stepped in through the covered walkway door. Wilson gave him a casual glance before adjusting his shirt collar.

"I want B256 and C26 to remain apart from each other," Abernathy instructed him. "If they get within five yards of each other, lock one up."

"Yep," Wilson uttered, feigning attention.

"The sooner Mr. Lanzendorf gets back, the better," Abernathy muttered to himself.

Wilson shot Abernathy a skeptical look and left for the common room.

Stupor took Abernathy's absence as a chance to stand up and wander over near Vengence.

"B256, what do you think you're doing?" Officer Herald called to him.

"Oh, just testing the waters," Stupor replied, quickly backing away as Vengence gave Stupor a flat stare.

"I bet you are. You need to stay away."

Stupor then shuffled his way over to Officer Herald, stopping just outside arm's reach. "Have you ever wondered why I waddle around and go 'blub, blub, blub' a lot?" he asked the guard.

"No, and I'm not particularly interested."

"Oh, okay. By the way, are you guys trained to act unfriendly or is it just a byproduct of being stuck under someone's thumb?"

Herald shot him a quick look and grumpily mumbled, "It's a byproduct, now go sit down."

"I get different answers from different kinds of people. I really like yours," Stupor beamed, backing away from Herald and giving a thumbs up.

As Stupor turned to walk away, he heard Wilson call out to him. "I need to have a word with you," he said as Stupor turned to face him. "Step outside, please."

Stupor obediently exited the building and followed Wilson a short ways from the door.

"You're a weird kid," Wilson said bluntly. "You have the whole security department talking about you. No one knows for sure if Lanzendorf got suspended because he's cracking or because you outsmarted the hell out of him. Personally, I think it's the latter."

"Why would you think that?" Stupor asked, his head cocked to the side.

"Mostly because I was there. I also think the rumors are true about you and C26 plotting to get him fired."

"Mr. Lanzendorf doesn't need my help to get fired," Stupor chuckled. "He does a great job of that all by himself."

"I don't expect you to trust me. I wouldn't if I were you. But even still I just want you to know that whatever it is that you're planning, as long as nobody's getting hurt I am willing to look the other way."

Stupor blinked his eyes in subtle confusion and said, "That's awfully shady."

"You remember Stacy Wilson, in medical? I

watched Lanzendorf make a threat against her life. Stacy is my daughter and whether he was serious or not, nobody talks to my little girl like that.

"I can't afford to lose my job so watching him get fired is the next best thing to taking my stun baton and sticking it up that asshole's asshole."

Stupor quietly nodded his head. He opened his mouth to say something, but was immediately cut off.

"Don't tell me what you're doing or even if you're doing anything at all," Wilson instructed, his brows furrowed. "You give me deniability and I'll give you silence. Now go back in there and I'll take care of Herald."

Stupor slowly turned and walked back into the common room. He boldly marched over to Vengence's table and sat down, looking directly at Officer Herald.

Herald moved to approach the two patients until Wilson called out to him. "Can this wait a few minutes? They're sitting together." he asked Wilson him impatiently.

"Let them talk," Wilson instructed.

"Abernathy said he wants them apart."

"Abernathy was demoted."

"But Lanzendorf said he's in charge."

Wilson gave Herald a stare and said, "There is no lead officer presently. I've been here longer than you and him combined and I say seniority rules. If they're not hurting anyone, I think we should just make our jobs easier."

Herald looked between Stupor and Officer Wilson, unsure of what to do.

"I'll take care of Abernathy," Wilson assured him. "He's nothing but a pretentious little kissass and I refuse to involve myself in their little B256 vendetta any more than necessary. You'd be wise to keep out of their games, too."

Herald gave a heavy sigh and returned to his post as Stupor smiled from underneath his mask.

***

"Well, things actually seem a lot better than I expected, now that Lanzendorf is away," Stupor said to Jörg as the two prepared for sleep.

"Das ist nicht überraschend. Glücklichsein macht alles einfacher," Jörg replied, laying on his back with his hands propped behind his head.

"Security seems pretty conflicted, too. Their individual dispositions are pretty interesting. It's stupidly easy to tell what they're really like just by the way they operate in a corrupt environment."

"Sie sind nur ein Rädchen in der Maschine wie jeder andere auch, das weißt du. Du kannst genauso gut dem Prozess die Kontrolle überlassen und dich zu deiner Bestimmung führen lassen."

"Well, I think I'm going to retire a little early, buddy. I'd love to keep chatting with you, but I'll be doing a lot of thinking on my feet tomorrow and I need my rest."

Jörg simply chuckled in response and rolled

over.

"Das Leben ist zu kurz, um ernst zu sein. Du hast dich sehr verändert, seitdem ich dich getroffen habe," he commented. "Was für ein Rätsel du bist! Trotzdem wirst du bald gelöst werden. Zu bald, meiner Meinung nach."

"Good night to you, too!"

***

"Is it possible to escape a spiral of destruction? Of course it is! Staying positive is the key. You just have to stop, turn ninety degrees, then go straight and punch right through the bad choices you've made. After that, you're free to start a brand new spiral.

"Life is a never ending web of bad choices. They're all bad because every single choice is a detriment to someone, either yourself or others. You selfish bastard."

***

In the security building, a lone guard named Officer Blake was sitting at the check-in counter. He looked up from reading a book to see Officer Abernathy enter.

"You're back already?" Blake asked him.

"I'm doing a double shift tonight, la-di-da," Abernathy grumbled. "I work overnight and then my typical morning shift."

"Gotta make that money, huh?"

"I need it. My landlord's been harping on me about rent again."

"I thought you lived at your parents' house?"

Abernathy looked up at him briefly and said, "Like I said: my landlord's harping on me about rent again."

Blake returned to reading his book, nodding his head. Abernathy punched in and moved into the CCTV room, gazing at the various monitors. Another guard, Officer Rodriguez, looked over at Abernathy from his office chair and waved prior to returning his attention to the screens.

"Anything interesting?" Abernathy asked.

"Nah. Everything's quiet as a church mouse," Rodriguez responded. "We got a nurse that came in about fifteen minutes ago. She said she's doing an extra half-shift."

"A half-shift? What does she look like?"

"Idunno, I only heard her talking out in the check-in room. She sounds cute though. Why?"

Without answering his question, Abernathy watched the screens attentively. In the medical building he saw one doctor and one nurse.

"Are you sure it wasn't Dr. Perez?" Abernathy inquired.

"Nope," responded Rodriguez. "Dr. Perez is salaried. She comes and goes whenever. No such thing as a shift for her."

"I know, it's just..." Abernathy responded, his sentence trailing off.

"Is everything okay?" the guard asked him, looking over with a concerned expression.

"Just make sure you keep an eye on those monitors, Rodriguez," he instructed, shaking his head. "Be alert, just in case. I'm going to see the living quarters."

Abernathy then walked to the check-in room and said to Blake, "I want you to ID every single person that comes in or out this entrance door, especially nurses."

"Something going on?" Blake asked him.

"I don't know yet. Just stay alert. I should be back soon."

Abernathy quickly made his way out of the security building and into the living quarters. He went straight upstairs toward Stupor's cell and looked inside his door.

There, he saw Stupor lying in bed. He lazily rolled over and tugged his blankets further up, exposing his bare feet.

Abernathy, unsure what to do, began pacing further down the hall. Reaching the end, he descended the stairs. As he reached the bottom floor, he doubled back and began moving toward the security building. Halfway down the hall, he heard his radio buzz.

"Abernathy, this is Rodriguez," it chirped. "I just saw a nurse entering the living quarters via the medical building's covered walkway. She just accessed the second floor hall."

"Ten-four," Abernathy affirmed.

He ran as quietly as he could muster back to the covered walkway entrance and up the stairs. At the top, he saw a nurse walking briskly down the hall, headed toward Stupor's cell. He silently scampered behind her, catching up. As he got close, he greeted, "Oh, hi there, ma'am!"

His acting was remarkably terrible and caused her to whip around quickly. She froze in place, staring at him.

"I didn't know who you were, but now I see that you're quite clearly a nurse here," Abernathy continued. "I'm, uh, just not really used to seeing medical personnel in the living quarters at this hour. But hey, I don't know what all you nurses do exactly, so yeah..."

Matching Stupor's description, she appeared to be Hispanic descent with medium-length black hair. Around her face she wore a medical mask.

"I'm working an extra half-shift," she replied. "I need the extra hours."

"Don't we all? Heh..." Abernathy quipped as he stepped closer to her. "So are overnight shifts as boring for you guys as it is for us?"

"I guess so," she replied with her eyes firmly fixed on him.

"I guess so, yep," Abernathy chuckled. "Well, I guess I'll be on my way. You have a nice night."

"Thanks, you too."

Abernathy nervously tried to move past her and once he was close enough, he grabbed her by her shirt with one hand. Before she could react, he used his other hand to rip off her medical mask, exposing her face. She stared back at him in utter dismay.

"I've got you, Dr. Perez–" he started before cutting his sentence short. The two stared at each other as he slowly realized her face was wholly unfamiliar to him. "You're not Dr. Perez..."

The woman then punched him hard in the groin, instantly loosening his grip. As Abernathy recoiled, she extracted a pepper spray bottle from her pocket and sprayed him in the face with it.

Abernathy cried out in pain as she made a mad dash past him for the stairs. His shouting began to wake the inmates as they peered out their door windows at him.

Abernathy made a bold attempt to run after her, fighting the intense searing pain that was coursing through his eyes. He staggered along as his vision blurred from a fiery combination of chemicals and tears.

"Get that stupid woman!" he shouted into the radio. "She ran toward the medical building entrance of the living quarters!"

Abernathy gave up before even reaching the stairs and sat down, propping himself against the wall. He wiped at his eyes as he listened to the radio chatter.

"CCTV shows her cutting through the courtyard, moving toward the common room."

"We see her. We're in pursuit."

"The woman's fast! Why can't she wear heels like the other nurses?!"

"All guards: she's in the maintenance building. How did she have access to it?! She's going out the other side!"

"We're on the perimeter moving in that direction."

"She has a moped out here! Was this organized?"

"She's gone! She's gone, damn it!"

"Don't call the police yet!" Abernathy barked into the radio. "I'm gonna call Lanzendorf right away! I repeat: do not call the police!"

Abernathy quickly pulled out his cell phone and mashed Lanzendorf's personal number into it. After a few moments of ringing, he picked up.

"What?!" Lanzendorf snapped, mildly groggy.

"Sir, that nurse came back and sprayed me in the eyes with pepper spray!" he sniveled.

"Are you seriously crying, Abernathy?" asked Lanzendorf with disgust.

"Pepper spray makes you cry, damn it!"

"No, you sound like a spanked child!"

"Sir, the nurse came back to the asylum!" Abernathy shouted, trying to change the subject. "The one that got shoved by C26!"

A deathly silence followed.

"She came back and was going toward B256's cell!" Abernathy continued blubbering through choked tears. "I stopped her and she hit me in the balls and then sprayed me with her pepper spray!"

"That scheming witch, I knew she was up to something!" Lanzendorf exclaimed. "She's taking advantage of my absence!"

"No, sir, it wasn't Dr. Perez! I was able to pull off her mask, she's someone I've never seen before!"

"Is her face on CCTV?"

"I don't know, I've got pepper spray in my

eyes!"

"Quit acting like a baby, Abernathy!"

Abernathy continued sniffling as Lanzendorf thought. After a moment he instructed, "Do not call the police. Have a guard post outside B256's cell at all times. Have him escorted wherever he needs to go. The woman is applying stealth. Our presence will be a visual deterrent."

"Can I go home for the night, sir?"

"No, you're stuck there. Work your double shift. Fill out an incident report and add some fluff about the police doing nothing. And stop crying!"

"Okay, but I'm not crying!" Abernathy lied before hanging up the phone.

He looked up and saw guards snickering as well as inmates looking out their doors, their eyes on him. He stood and was about to speak when his phone rang. Seeing it was Lanzendorf calling, he answered.

"You do not hang up on me, I hang up on you!" Lanzendorf shouted before abruptly ending the call.

Abernathy wobbled past the guards with an angry, embarrassed frown. Meanwhile, Stupor sat inside his cell, curled up in the far corner of his bed and trembling in terror.

Chapter Eleven

"Warst du die ganze Nacht wach?" Jörg asked as he looked up at Stupor, sitting upright and cross-legged.

"I am totally scared out of my wits, man," Stupor said to him, slightly groggy.

"Viel Glück. Der letzte Akt beginnt!" Jörg exclaimed with a laugh, patting Stupor's knee.

Stupor watched Jörg happily leave the cell and elected to remain on his bed. He pulled his legs close and gazed at the courtyard through his room's window.

The badger stared at him with warm, inviting eyes. It didn't move from its place next to Stupor on the couch, but he knew in his heart it was alive. Its face was oddly wide, almost cartoonish in form. Stupor questioned whether or not it was a badger at all, but knew in his heart it was so. As he reached out to pet it, it nibbled on his fingers affectionately.

Stupor, realizing he was asleep, jolted himself awake and looked about his cell frightenedly. He smacked the top of his head a couple times and gazed out the window once more.

Officer Wilson curiously peered inside and looked at Stupor. "Are you planning on eating breakfast?" he asked.

"I'm scared that woman's waiting for me out there!" Stupor responded.

"Who do you know that hates you so much they want to kill you?"

"I have no idea! I've been in here for over a year! How do I make enemies from in here?"

"Idunno," Wilson answered, shrugging. "But you now have twenty-four hour protection as per Lanzendorf's orders, so you can at least sleep and exit your cell now comfortably."

Stupor sighed and climbed out of bed.

"I don't even feel much like blubbing today," he commented, putting on slippers and exiting the cell.

He meandered his way to the common room and grabbed some breakfast. Just after sitting at Vengence's table, he was approached by Officer Abernathy.

"You need to get away from C26," he told Stupor.

"Let them talk," Wilson told him.

Abernathy looked at him with surprise and asserted, "I want them to remain apart."

"I think the he had a stressful experience last night and deserves to be able to talk to any peer he feels comfortable around. If there's a problem with that, we can always consult Dr. Perez or Dr. Goodrich about how much they're able to get patient C26 to talk to anybody."

Abernathy gave Stupor and Wilson a critical look.

"What are they going to do, scheme with me around?" Wilson asked, his hands on his hips. "Go back to your post; I have everything under control here."

"I'm the lead officer," Abernathy shot back.

"There is no lead officer here; you're just an extension of Lanzendorf's authority. Might I also add that Lanzendorf currently has zero authority. I am the senior officer here and I'm running the show."

"You didn't say that yesterday, Wilson!"

"I also didn't burst into tears like a momma's boy because of some pepper spray, because that would not be very becoming of a leader."

Abernathy gave a furious glare and stomped away, extracting his cell phone from his pocket.

"You all have until Lanzendorf comes back," Wilson muttered to the two barons. "After that, we're all screwed." Wilson then stepped a short distance away so he couldn't hear any discussion.

Stupor looked at the common room entrance and saw Ralph enter, stumbling past Abernathy. Abernathy gave him a disgusted look in passing. Stupor immediately got up and intercepted him.

Ralph was in the exact same clothing from the previous day, though it was matted down with dark green and brown stains. His face was completely covered in cigarette ashes, his hair shiny with an unknown oily substance.

"I got your coffee," Ralph said slowly, looking slightly to Stupor's left.

"Wow, thanks! I completely forgot that asked for this, Ralph!" Stupor happily replied. "What took you so long?"

"Nobody made any coffee until this morning. I waited until they did."

"Huh. Well, thanks for the strong effort, my

friend!"

As Stupor extended his hand to receive the coffee, he was knocked aback by a putrid rotten fish smell coming from Ralph.

"Good gravy!" Stupor exclaimed, recoiling. "What kind of crap did you swim in?"

Ralph examined his clothes and shrugged his shoulders. "I think I spilled the coffee creamer," he explained, then licked his lips. "I got you your coffee."

Stupor uneasily took the coffee, which was oddly ice cold. "What about the organization of the security guards?" he asked Ralph. "Did you figure that out for me?"

"Oh... I don't know how to do that," Ralph replied, then turned to walk away.

"Ralph! Wait!"

Ralph lazily stopped, turned, and approached Stupor again. He then stared at Stupor's mask, breathing heavily. "I'm really tired," he protested weakly.

"I heard about a passdown form Lanzendorf made for the other guards. Could you make a copy of that and bring it to me before lunch?"

"Yeah, I'll do it."

Ralph then walked away. Several employees were repelled by his smell as he passed. Stupor returned to Vengence's table, placing the coffee in the trash can en route.

"I'd rather not take my chances on Ralph's coffee," Stupor said to Vengence, trailing off into a light chuckle.

Vengence simply looked out the window.

"So Vengence... are you sure you can't help me get rid of this woman that wants me dead?" Stupor asked earnestly.

"That is correct," Vengence answered coldly, maintaining his focus on the window. "Kill her if she is a thorn in your side, but do it honorably."

"I can't do that if I don't know where she is!"

"You might if you escaped from here."

"I want to keep myself safe without becoming a fugitive of the law, Mr. Sir!"

"That is not my name, Baron Von Stupor," Vengence commented. "Though it is a welcome break from Vengence."

Stupor lay his head down, pouting. "Wanna play another game of chess?" he asked after a pause.

"Negative. What are we doing as far as escape is concerned?"

"Idunno. I'm hoping I'll know after a while." Stupor muttered in response.

***

"If the body wants something bad enough, it takes it. Humans fight for their individuality, but in the end are just as selfish as any predatory animal searching for whatever meal it can. The only difference is that humans aren't always after primal needs. This makes them so much more dangerous.

"This acknowledgment and insight is what fuels our ability to fight that primal selfishness and form the

coherent society we have today. Some can fight it more than others, and others fight it all too well, ironically leading to their own self-destruction. Oh well. In the end we're only human, right?"

"POTATOPOTATOPOTATO–"

***

Stupor was sharply awakened by the putrid smell of dead fish and cinnamon-laced oatmeal. Before he could know what was going on, he felt himself gagging.

As he awoke, Ralph stood before him placing a sheet of paper on the table. His clothes were sopping wet as green chunks of an unidentifiable substance dripped down from them. His face was totally blackened from more cigarette ashes.

"How the hell have you not been sent home, boy?!" Wilson berated while standing far away.

The inmates were all complaining from afar and Vengence had retreated to another corner of the room.

Stupor snatched the sheet of paper off the table and stumbled away, retching violently. He looked behind him and saw the other security guards looking onward, unsure of how best to approach Ralph.

Everyone yelled at him to leave as he looked around, distressed and confused. He clapped his hands over his ears hard and ran out the door, clipping the frame on the way out and falling to the floor. In all of a moment he was at his feet and gone from the room.

Stupor looked at the paper Ralph gave him and quickly realized it was a badly handwritten replica of the security building's passdown form. Noting that the grammar and spelling were fine throughout, he accepted the copy as legitimate and quickly read it.

"Give me that paper right now," Abernathy demanded.

"It's private," Stupor told him. "Stop being so nosy!"

"You need to let me see that. As per asylum policy, any notes that are not delivered through the postal system can be subject to seizure and screening by security."

"How about this?" Stupor asked, tearing the folded paper in half and holding one piece out. "What if we split it fifty-fifty?"

Abernathy gave him a flat look and stepped toward Stupor, attempting to grab at the paper scrap. Stupor backed away and promptly shoved it underneath his mask and into his mouth.

"Om, nom, nom," Stupor said aloud. "Can I go to solitary now?"

Abernathy glared at Stupor and gestured for the two guards at the entrance for assistance. They along with a couple orderlies surrounded Stupor and closed in. Stupor manipulated their arms and squeezed his way through, swallowing the paper and shoving the other half into his mouth. He briefly paused to gag on the first half as it slid slowly down his throat.

"Always eat your fiber!" Stupor choked while wagging his finger.

The entire group came after him once more, surrounding him. Stupor allowed himself to be caught and swallowed the second piece of paper before they had a chance to pull it out.

"So do I get to go to solitary now?" he asked Abernathy as he was restrained with his hands behind his back.

"Shut up!" Abernathy shot back and looked to the two guards. "Bring him into my office!"

"That kid really knows how to make a weird scene come out of nowhere," Wilson said out loud as Stupor was escorted out of the building.

***

"Now I know exactly how Lanzendorf feels when you keep trying to make a fool out of him," Abernathy said, pacing and fuming. "And you sure seem to love doing it."

"Nah," Stupor said, fiddling with his wrist restraints. "I just needed to buy enough time to eat the paper so you couldn't read it."

"What's so important about that paper that you needed to eat it?"

"To be honest, the paper itself didn't become important until you wanted to take it from me. Can I go to solitary now?"

Abernathy shot him a glare.

"You're actually asking for solitary?" he asked rhetorically. "You probably need it for a reason, right? Well, I'm not going to give you what you want. In fact, I have a better idea. We're gonna go for a walk."

"I think I'd rather go into solitary," Stupor uttered, feeling a lump in his throat.

"No. Let's go for a walk. Just a short one."

Oh dear, Stupor thought to himself. *This isn't what I wanted.*

Abernathy spoke into his radio and within moments a couple muscular guards entered the room. Stupor read their nametags and identified them as Officers Grant and Myers.

Stupor was then escorted out of the building via the check-in room and into the employee parking lot. They continued to walk him through the lot and into the yard slightly around the complex perimeter. Just after reaching the other side of the security building, they stopped with Grant and Myers holding Stupor by either arm.

"As I'm sure you're aware, Mr. Lanzendorf has a special place where he takes problematic inmates," Abernathy explained as Stupor glanced at the nearby employee access road and toward the dense forest that decorated the other side of it. "He has his own brand of rehabilitation that he employs when he can't control someone. He normally uses it on chronically violent patients, to curb their behavior more effectively. The most important thing to him is one hundred percent compliance.

"Out here there are no cameras. No one will ever know what we do. These two gentlemen, hand-picked by Mr. Lanzendorf, specifically work in tandem on Sundays. One might know them as Mr. Lanzendorf's 'enforcers.' As fate might have it, Sundays are also one of the two days of the week that the entire board of directors is off."

"If I may interject," Stupor cut in. "If you bring violent inmates out here, then why me?"

"Well, let me think about some of the things that have happened to me over the past couple days," Abernathy mused, his leering becoming more intense. "I have been humiliated countless times in front of coworkers and inmates, I have been pepper sprayed, and I have been hit in my balls. Oh yes, and I've been demoted. I really got it from Mom when that happened. Yes, we normally bring violent inmates out here for 'special treatment', but for you I'm making an exception.

"You see, I have worked too freaking hard to get where I'm at and I am not going to let you come in and just act like you're the champion of the inmates. This is my chance to step up to the plate and show Mr. Lanzendorf that I have what it takes to run the show!

"So, B256, this is how it's going to work. Mr. Lanzendorf is not a stupid guy. You and C26 are plotting something. I want to know what your plan is and what was written on that paper you got from Ralph. If you don't, I will have no choice but to force it out of you."

"You know you're taking a huge risk," Stupor commented. "What about after I go back inside?

Won't you guys get fired or something?"

"I'm going to be perfectly honest with you. You were nothing more than a pipsqueak to me the whole time you've been here. After you got Mr. Lanzendorf suspended the other day, that's when I really recognized you for the threat he always said you were.

"You're really sneaky, really intelligent, really cunning... I realize that now. So now I hate you the same way he does because you're a disruption to the amazing system Mr. Lanzendorf created."

"There's not much you can do about it if you get fired!" Stupor argued. "Your mom is gonna spank you bad!"

"Stop talking about my mom!" Abernathy shouted. "And I'm not gonna get fired!"

"If you say so, Mr. Abernathzendorf."

"Hold him tight, guys," Abernathy said to the guards, who then strengthened their grip. "This guy's a worm, but we'll teach him just like the others."

Abernathy backed up and began to loosen his shoulders and neck. He then balled up his fists and threw an underhanded punch toward Stupor's gut. Stupor quickly twisted to the side and raised his leg, deflecting the blow with his knee. Abernathy nodded confidently and threw another punch, aimed right at Stupor's sternum. Stupor responded by quickly dropping himself and thrusting his head downward, butting the top of Abernathy's hand. Abernathy jerked away and shook his hand in pain.

As Abernathy looked back to Stupor, Stupor stood and swung his head to the left and right, smacking Grant and Myers on their foreheads with the tips of the horns on his mask. As they flinched, Stupor completely lifted his legs, gravity snatching his arms free from the guards' grasp and landing on his rear.

Stupor then rolled back and brought himself to his feet as the two guards lunged at him, their arms extended. Stupor reacted by concentrating his backward momentum into a back flip. As his feet rose into the air, they accidentally hit the guards' hands. Disoriented, Stupor barely stuck his landing. After stumbling slightly, he quickly ran along the side of the building. He hurriedly worked his way around the facility with the three officers in hot pursuit.

"Don't let him get away or else we're dead!" he heard Abernathy shout frantically as the trio chased Stupor as fast as they could.

Before too long, Stupor approached the main driveway of the asylum and stood before the front door. He turned backwards and opened the door with his restrained hands, then twirled inward, allowing the door to shut behind him. He looked at the check-in counter and saw a very surprised receptionist.

"Hello, ma'am," Stupor greeted. "The guards are taking me for a walk outside the asylum, but I wanted to make sure it was okay with you first."

Just as he finished his sentence, Abernathy, Grant, and Myers burst in through the door and tackled him to the ground.

***

Officer Abernathy sank deep in a chair inside the office of Mr. Bark as the director stared a hole through his head in a quiet rage.

"You took him outside and he escaped?" Mr. Bark asked cynically.

"Y-yes," Abernathy answered, beginning to sweat bullets. "He viciously attacked us and ran away. You've seen that he can fight."

"Did this assault leave any marks?"

"They-they're gone now. Except I do have a scratch on my knuckles," Abernathy blathered, lifting his hand to show a pathetic abrasion on his middle finger. "He headbutted my hand."

Mr. Bark gave his hand a brief, unimpressed glance, then returned to meet his nervous gaze, his face glowing with rage. "According to the security footage I watched," he mentioned. "he left the check-in room in restraints. Regardless of why you took him out, nearly ten whole minutes later he entered the welcome building door still restrained. How exactly would you explain that, Mr. Abernathy?"

"He, um..." Abernathy stammered, his brows raised. "I-I don't know how to explain that."

"You can't explain how while in restraints he assaulted three security guards outside, ran away, and then re-entered the facility without trying to escape?"

Abernathy sat in deep thought for a moment and answered, "He's crazy. You never know what they can or will do, right?"

"Incorrect," Mr. Bark responded, his voice becoming increasingly livid. "Did you know, Mr. Abernathy, that he could have easily escaped the asylum if he ran toward the woods?" Mr. Bark was practically shouting by this point. "Do you know what kinds of ramifications would occur if an involuntarily committed patient escaped? Do you know what kind of impact that would have on our review coming in just a few months?"

Abernathy broke eye contact and stared at Mr. Bark's nameplate resting at the edge of his desk.

"If patient B256 attacked you and ran away, then you were ignorant and negligent," Mr. Bark spat. "If this is not actually what happened, you were being deceitful and contrary to everything the security force in this facility should stand for."

Mr. Bark pulled out a sheet of carbon paper and wrote in silence. Abernathy leaned forward to see what was being written, but could not due to the angle. Mr. Bark did not seem to notice.

After a few minutes, Mr. Bark slapped the paper down in front of him along with a pen and instructed, "Please read this entire sheet and sign your acknowledgment at the bottom."

Abernathy looked down at the sheet and turned pale. "T-termination?" he uttered.

"You're lucky that boy is honest," Mr. Bark

commented. "Things would be far, far worse for you—legally—if he actually tried to run away from the facility."

Abernathy gave a half-hearted signature and returned the paper. Mr. Bark then grumpily tore off the pink copy and gave it to Abernathy prior to waving dismissively.

"Have all of your things out of here by close of business," he said without looking up from his desk.

Abernathy trod outside, feeling a giant lump emerging in his throat. He sulked from the office to the courtyard, reading his pink slip over and over again. Halfway to the security building, he pulled out his phone and called Lanzendorf.

"What do you want, Abernathy?" Lanzendorf irritably asked from the other end.

"They fired me, sir," he blubbered into the phone, barely able to contain himself.

"They what?! What happened?!"

"I was running the place just like you do, sir! I kept the patients in check and the guards on task, and then Wilson started acting like he was in charge because he's the senior."

"Get to the point!"

"Well, B256 kept acting up and asking to go into solitary. Well, I wasn't gonna give him what he wanted, just like you! So I took him outside and I was just gonna rough him up a bit."

"You took him outside?!"

"I took Grant and Myers with me! It should have been okay!" Abernathy was by then sobbing and hiccuping with every few words.

"You took that risk knowing full well what he's capable of?" Lanzendorf raged. "What were you thinking, you idiot?"

"I was just trying to impress you!"

"Well congratulations, you got yourself fired instead! Never call me again, you moron!"

Lanzendorf hung up on Abernathy just as the blubbering former employee reached the security building's covered walkway entrance.

"I tried to tell you that you'd get fired, but nope!" Stupor spouted from a short ways away. He stood pompously, holding his hands on his hips. "Nope, don't listen to me! I'm just a crazy guy in a mask! Hey, are you gonna eat that pink slip? I could use some extra fiber."

"Why are you being so mean?" Abernathy asked, his eyes red with tears.

"Because you're a bully," Stupor said in quick reply. "And I make sure bullies get what's coming to them, every time."

Abernathy thought to himself for a moment, his eyes toward the ground. He then nodded his head at Stupor before entering the building.

***

"I haven't seen him at all since," Stupor said to Jörg, who raised his eyebrows impressedly.

"Er ist so gut wie weg. Gute Arbeit!" Jörg complimented, shooting Stupor a thumbs up. "Ich freue mich darauf, deine nächste Geschichte zu hören. Ich hoffe, ich komme darin vor!"

"I really didn't want him to get fired, but some people just need a black eye or two before they open their eyes. Knocking someone off their high horse needs a little bit of participation from the little man, you know."

Jörg scratched his chin, then smiled brightly. Stupor lay in his bed and stared at the ceiling.

The wind of change is blowing, he thought to himself. *Good or bad, I feel myself moving forward only. Ergo, I am strangely content.*

***

"I hope you feel proud of yourself."

"Not yet. Wait, who is this?"

"Cactus!"

"Cactus?"

"CACTUS!"

click

Chapter Twelve

The following morning, Stupor scurried to the common room as soon as he could to meet with Vengence. Just as yesterday, he was escorted by Officer Wilson.

"So with little Abernathy gone, management recognizes me as the official senior officer until the new lead officer is named," Wilson said to him. "I put my own name in for what it's worth, but this is good enough."

"Congratulations, good sir Wilson!" Stupor complimented.

"I really don't condone workplace grudges, but I have to admit you've made me a bit more proud of the work I do here over the past few days."

"I'm not chasing any grudges," Stupor said. "I'm just trying to live my life as normally as any involuntary patient can!"

A miniscule chuckle escaped Wilson as the two arrived at Vengence's table. As usual, Wilson stepped out of hearing range.

"I must get to the patient storage area before I escape," Vengence mentioned to Stupor. "It is crucial that I retrieve my effects before leaving."

"I hear that. I really miss my cope," Stupor empathized. Noticing Vengence's confused look, he added, "It looks like a coat, but it's so much more!"

"My effects have no sentimental value to me," Vengence denied, losing all interest in Stupor's invented vocabulary. "When I was placed in this rat cage, I had some of my technology confiscated from me. I cannot allow it to stay, as it does not belong in this time period."

"Oh, like what?"

"You only need to know that I must retrieve my effects or escape is pointless."

Stupor shuffled his feet as he casually looked around the room.

"She is not here," Vengence muttered. "Stop distracting yourself."

"That's a relief," Stupor replied with a sigh. "I hope she got bored with attempted murder. It's an irritating hobby when you're the target."

"She has not been here ever since yesterday morning. After being spotted a second time, I would expect anyone of moderate intelligence to stay away."

"How come you're suddenly helping me with advice again?"

"Your paranoia is only slightly more agitating than your flagrant contraction usage. If you were wise, you would not criticize my unwarranted generosity."

"Not at all, buddy! Thanks!"

Vengence growled and looked at the guards, who seemed bored. Stupor was surprised as Jörg suddenly tapped him on his shoulder.

"Du bist das größte Mysterium überhaupt," he said, smiling enormously. "Jedes Mal, wenn einer denkt, er hat dein Rätsel gelöst, passiert etwas, was das ganze Spiel verändert! Deine

Freunde, deine Intelligenz und sogar die Naturgewalten! Ich bin so glücklich, dass ich dich getroffen habe."

Jörg then gave Stupor a big thumbs up and swiftly walked away. Stupor wondered what Jörg was talking about until he noticed the time.

"Oh man! I need to get to my appointment!" he exclaimed. "Jörg must have been warning me about that. I've really lost track of the days lately! See you later, Vengence!"

As Stupor got up, Vengence quickly grabbed him and pulled him close. "Tomorrow we shall finalize our plan. Tomorrow night I escape," he asserted.

"S-so soon?" Stupor asked in surprise.

"Yes. I cannot stand this place any longer and we have no way to know how long this window of opportunity will be open. No one suspects our plan, so tomorrow night we will act."

"I—well... Okay then."

Vengence narrowed his eyes at Stupor. "You sound unsure."

"I'm just not really ready yet!"

"That is why we finalize the plan tomorrow and then I escape tomorrow night. Remember: you are in or out. I am making my move with or without you."

Stupor nodded his head in acknowledgment before heading off to his appointment, escorted by Officer Wilson.

***

"Baron Von Stupor, you've certainly been the talk of the town," Dr. Goodrich commented as Stupor sat in a chair.

"Oh really? I hope you've said only good things about me!" Stupor replied with a swing of his arm.

Dr. Goodrich smirked and revealed Stupor's file. He opened it up and shuffled some papers around.

"So how are you feeling today?" he asked, looking at Stupor with interest.

"I guess I'm okay. I'm still a tiny bit paranoid about that nurse that wants to kill me. Vengence told me she hasn't been around lately though, so I've been more comfortable."

"That's good," Dr. Goodrich acknowledged, scribbling on a notepad. "How has the recent absence of Mr. Lanzendorf made you feel?"

"At first I felt empty inside, like something important in my life had suddenly gone missing," Stupor described, adjusting his weight in the chair. "But that's when Officer Abernathy started turning into a sort of store brand version of Mr. Lanzendorf.

"Everything started to feel normal again until he got fired. Now everything feels so... peaceful. It's almost like respect and dignity are slowly returning to the facility.

"If you ask me, I think this is a serious issue and we need to act on this before patients start saying they like the place."

Dr. Goodrich blinked his eyes in confusion and uttered, "Officer Abernathy is a store brand version of Mr. Lanzendorf?"

"Yeah! Like if Lanzendorf were a breakfast cereal, I imagine he'd be called something sorta like 'Lanzen Puffs'. And then Officer Abernathy would be something like 'Abernastee-O's', but the cereal would still be puff-shaped.

"Then if I called the cereal company to ask about it they'd be like 'They're totally shaped like O's. Just imagine the O's if they had no holes. Absernastee-O's!'"

"That's certainly a new one," Dr. Goodrich said, continuing to write notes. "Did you prepare that before you came here today?"

"Yeah," Stupor admitted with a laugh.

"Alright, well I've heard enough about that," Dr. Goodrich commented without looking up from his pad. "I'd like to touch up on an older topic of ours."

"What's there to touch up on?"

"I'd like you to elaborate on how you came up with the name Baron Von Stupor."

"You sure like hearing about that lately."

"That name is where everything started, and I would like to think that every time we discuss it I unravel a little more truth behind it."

"Oh, really?" Stupor asked, sitting up in his seat. "What kinds of truths have you unraveled so far?"

"I'm not sure if you really want me to answer that or not," Dr. Goodrich replied, interlacing his fingers and looking at Stupor with slight contempt.

"Oh, come on. Don't make a guy curious!"

"Well, for the past few months I have actually been collecting these stories of yours," the doctor began, gathering together Stupor's files. "You tell me something very different in each story and yet they all seem to have one connection: Your name always comes into play after some inconvenience that happened to you, an accident that you had absolutely no control over."

"Huh. Every story?" Stupor asked, impressed. "That's very weird and unintentional."

"Personally, I think you thrive on receiving attention," the doctor continued, suddenly stern. "However, you're more intelligent than that. You want certain kinds of attention from certain people. When you want someone to be friends, they're just warming up to you if they get angry. When you want to be the victim, someone else is always to blame."

"I actually have a—"

"When you want to be enigmatic, you evade the answers to questions," the doctor continued, completely bowling Stupor over. "And when you want people to place you in a mental hospital and take care of you courtesy of the people's tax dollars, you exploit the system. Stupor, I really do think you are emotionally disturbed. Perhaps you were neglected by your adoptive parents when you were growing up. However, I have absolutely no notion that you belong here and once I have a sufficient case of malingering to present, I will see that the board of directors is made aware of it."

The two sat among an awkward silence. Dr. Goodrich stared into the eyes of Stupor's mask as Stupor stared back, his hand clasped and his legs straight.

"Now, Stupor, what were you going to say?" Dr. Goodrich asked.

"I forgot," answered Stupor, with a shrug of his shoulders. "It's why I tried to interrupt you!"

"Did you actually forget what you wanted to say or are you faking that, too?"

"I'm probably faking that too, to be honest, but I'm honeslty not sure. Hey, can I get some water? You really should try to get a refrigerator in here. Stock some sodas, man!"

Stupor got up and stepped out of the room as Dr. Goodrich rubbed the bridge of his nose. After a moment, Stupor returned to his chair, a water bottle in hand.

"Okay, where were we again?" he asked after fighting to take a drink under his mask without spilling it.

"You were just about to say something, but conveniently forgot," Dr. Goodrich reminded.

"Oh right! How is your wife? Is she going to bring brownies again?"

Dr. Goodrich thought for a moment, then looked at a photo on his desk he had recently flipped face-down. He angrily snatched it and dropped it into a desk drawer before slapping the drawer shut. He then shot a nasty glare at Stupor and spat, "You are such an insensitive, conniving bastard."

"Takes one to know one, you know," Stupor deadpanned, getting up. "But hey, thanks for the water! Same time Wednesday, right? I'll talk to Michala at the desk about it."

Stupor left the room, took a few steps, then leaned back to stick his head in Dr. Goodrich's doorway. The doctor remained at his chair, his face buried in his hands.

"Hey, Dr. Goodrich?" Stupor asked. "Could you please treat me a little more professionally? You're really smart and analytical, but you've gotten pretty mean lately, like your emotions are getting the best of you. Keep the personal stuff at home, man!

"I'm no psychiatrist, but I have a feeling that patient trust is kind of a job requirement, and you're definitely not going to get any if you're calling people names. You kinda hurt my feelings today, but don't tell anyone I told you."

"Just please leave," Dr. Goodrich said calmly without lifting his head.

Stupor obediently left, shaking his head in disappointment.

***

"Your personal enemies are making my life very difficult," Vengence complained to Stupor in the common room after hearing what he read from the passdown form. “Locks resetting each shift? Everyone being buzzed into the security building? You have single-handedly escalated this facility to medium-security.”

“Hey now,” Stupor argued. “It’s still an open unit.”

Vengence leered at Stupor and returned his full attention to the guards.

“We need at least one security building guard to access the security building itself,” Vengence continued. “We must get his card during the same shift in which I escape.”

“Actually, Mr. Lanzendorf’s window is a great point of access since you already smashed the crap out of it!” Stupor reminded him.

“If the security staff is any form of intelligent they will have guards post at Lanzendorf’s office for that exact reason.”

“Wouldn’t it be easier for you to beat up those guards instead of trying to go through the front door?”

“Getting me past the front door is supposed to be your specialty,” Vengence asserted, jabbing his finger at him. “You gave me access to that building before; you need to do it again.”

“Well, pickpocketing a key card from a guard in the security building while in my cell... it’s kind of hard!”

“Hmph,” Vengence grunted in disapproval. He then leaned back in his chair and crossed his arms.

“What if we just cause another riot?” Stupor

asked, his finger tapping his chin. "It will attract all available guards and you can slip in through Mr. Lanzendorf's window!"

"Leave the window out of this!" Vengence snapped. "I cannot use the window as the guards posted there will not be 'available' to assist their peers with a riot! Furthermore, we will not be able to start a riot as the inmates cannot get out of their cells!"

"You know, we could actually get the cells open if—"

"Even if we started our plan in the living quarters, the guards would be alerted long before we were inside the security building," Vengence continued, cutting him off. "We need to find a way to get closer to the security building before we make our move."

"So how do I get closer to a security building guard?"

"Get yourself to solitary. Get the card on the way there, then run away. Open my door, give the card to me, and I will make my escape. We can fight the guards together."

"I think you're overrating my fighting skills a little bit," Stupor said uncomfortably. "I'm not exactly a one man army!"

"I entirely expect you to be overwhelmed. I will use their distraction to my advantage and enter the security building. While you distract the guards, I will retrieve my effects and escape this damned rat hole."

"Your plan throws me under the bus."

"You chose not to escape," Vengence coldly reminded him with crossed arms. "I do not need your help beyond that point, therefore sacrificing yourself is objectively more beneficial. I feel like I should also remind you that I do not need your help in the first place. You are only here to make my escape easier."

"Meh," Stupor whined, crossing his arms. "I better not get beat up, Vengence! And you're lucky we're friends!"

"We are not friends."

***

"Hey!" Stupor exclaimed, entering the group therapy room. "You're not Dr. Goodrich!"

"Hello Stupor," Dr. Perez chuckled. "I'll be holding the group therapy session tonight. Dr. Goodrich went home early today."

Stupor recoiled in surprise and asked, "Was it an emergency or something?"

"I'm sorry, but I'm not at liberty to say. I'll make sure he knows you were concerned about him."

She then turned around and assisted the rest of the patients into the room. Vengence entered and walked past her without responding to her friendly greeting.

He sat in a chair in the farthest corner of the room. Noticing this, Stupor got out of his seat and moved to sit near him.

"You follow me like a duckling," Vengence

groaned.

"Yakkity quack!" Stupor chirped in response.

All patients gradually entered the room and found their seats without issue. Many watched Dr. Perez curiously while others seemed more preoccupied with talking to each other. Everyone became quiet as soon as Dr. Perez shut the door.

"Dr. Goodrich has gone home early today, so I will be substituting him for the evening," she announced to the group with a smile on her face. "I have an activity here that Dr. Goodrich has planned, so I assure you that my presence here will not affect his typical procedure in any way."

She then walked over to a small table on the other side of the room and picked up a large plastic soda bottle.

"Today he wants us to play a variation of the 'Spin the Bottle' game," she continued. "There is a plus and a minus on either side of this bottle. We will take turns spinning the bottle. When it stops, the person who the plus points at will share a little bit about their strengths. Then, the person with the minus will share some of their work areas."

"Work areas?" Vengence suddenly asked in a cynical tone.

"Yes," Dr. Perez answered. "Work areas are things about yourself that you feel could use improvement."

"One of the largest Terran work areas is their overuse of inoffensive terminology. Stupid terms like 'work areas' instead of referring to them by their true name: weaknesses."

"We don't anyone to feel less comfortable about themselves or feel like they are weak just because of something about them that could use improvement. We work on these areas, so they are work areas."

"If one cannot perform to the standards expected of them, they are weak. If they are any kind of true warrior, their pride should inspire them to overcome. Denying a weakness is true weakness."

"We call them work areas because not every work area is a weakness."

"If we are not discussing weakness, then why is there a minus on that bottle, woman? Do not try and wind your words around me."

"The minus is just a symbol, Mr. Vengence."

"The symbols represent two opposing forces: good and bad. Strength and weakness. Pride and shame. There is nothing in between. You do not want us to discuss work areas that are not also weaknesses. These symbols represent your desire for us to acknowledge where we are weak.

"Do not try to sugarcoat us like we are still freshborn slugs, yearning for maternal love. If the people in this room cannot handle the truth of their weakness, then they are a disgrace to their kind."

Dr. Perez stared at Vengence with impatience for a moment, then said, "Thank you for sharing your opinion, Mr. Vengence. We appreciate that you are willing to give us your attention."

"Way to go, buddy!" Stupor spoke, giving Vengence's arm a friendly pat with the back of his hand. "You're finally opening up!"

Vengence flashed an angry look at Stupor before sitting back in his seat. Paul gazed from his own seat at Vengence in admiration of his outburst. The other patients appeared largely uncomfortable with Vengence's presence.

"I'll spin first," Dr. Perez informed the group as she brought a small table to the center of their circle. "Whoever receives the minus does not have to share, but if they do, they get to spin next. If they do not share, then the spinning privileges will defer to the patient who received the plus."

Dr. Perez then lightly spun the bottle. After a few moments, it slowed to a halt with the plus pointing to Terry Rogers and the minus pointing to Paul Galliver.

"Alright, Terry," Dr. Perez continued. "Feel free to share with us some of your strengths."

"Well," Terry replied with a smirk. "I'm very strong inside and outside. I have a lot of pride. Nobody messes with me! And when I really want something, I can get it!"

Vengence scoffed, inciting a glare from Terry.

"You have a problem, big guy?" he asked condescendingly.

"You are far more deluded than any other Terran," Vengence responded without looking at him. "Your only worth is found inside a fighter jet."

Terry's jaw dropped and his face reddened.

"You are really asking for it!" he threatened. "If you had any hair, I'd come over there and slap it right off!"

Vengence turned and looked at him with narrow eyes.

"Fly away, fighter pilot," he mocked.

"What is with you and calling me a fighter pilot? It doesn't make any sense!"

"Guys, I think we should settle down," Dr. Perez softly reprimanded the two. "Terry, you've shared your strengths. Now it's Paul's turn to share his work areas."

Vengence released a loud, impatient sigh.

"I can't trust anyone here," Paul commented, looking between Stupor and Vengence. "I don't know if we're all patients or if the patients are just part of the elaborate scheme to hold me here. I just wish I knew who's on my side."

Dr. Perez finished writing some notes on a pad and said, "Thank you for sharing that, Paul. You can spin next."

Paul gave the bottle a half-hearted spin. It landed with the plus sign facing a patient named Jade Morris and the minus facing Stupor.

"Jade, would you like to share some of your strengths?" Dr. Perez asked her.

"I, uh..." she replied sheepishly. "I can't really think of anything."

"It's okay, you can take a moment to think. There's no rush."

After a brief thought, Jade said to the group,

"Well, I really like photography."

"So would you say that you're creative and artistic?" the doctor asked.

"Yeah, I guess so," Jade answered with a weak smile.

"That's very nice. I hope you get a chance to explore that creativity of yours. Thank you for sharing that."

Jade simply nodded her head and looked to the floor sheepishly.

"And Stupor," Dr. Perez continued. "are you interested in sharing a work area?"

"I distract everyone with my ruggedly good looks!" Stupor responded with his chest puffed out.

Vengence rolled his eyes as the rest of the group took a moment to chuckle.

"How about a serious work area?" Dr. Perez continued patiently. "Is there something you'd like to share about yourself that you feel could use improvement?"

"No, but I wanna spin that bottle," Stupor answered reluctantly. The doctor watched quietly as he thought to himself. "Well... I don't know if this is a work area or not but I don't like change very much, especially when it's me that changes. And in order to have more friends, I would have to change more toward something people would want to be friends with. But I like myself just the way I am, so I say poo on change! Change stinks! Except that leaves me stuck with just Jörg and Vengence. No offense, guys!"

"We are absolutely not friends!" a grouchy Vengence reminded him as Jörg gave a thumbs up.

Dr. Perez thought to herself for a moment, then wrote something down on her pad.

"Thank you, Stupor. Now it's your turn to spin the bottle," she instructed him.

"What did you write on your pad?" Stupor asked.

"I wrote that you have few friends."

"You only got that much out of what I said? Well, okay then."

"What did you want me to get from it?" Dr. Perez asked as he accidentally spun the bottle off of the small table. "Is there something you'd like me to know?"

"Meh," he replied inattentively. "You're the doctor; you know what's more important in the things people say."

Dr. Perez looked curious and concerned as Stupor picked up the bottle and spun it again, managing to keep it on the table. It landed with the plus pointing at Vengence and the minus at Jörg.

"Vengence, would you like to share some of your strengths?" Dr. Perez asked him.

"I am stronger, faster, and smarter than any organism in this room," Vengence said, shooting a nasty look at her. "My strength is that I am universally superior."

"Vengence, you will not be able to participate in these activities if you are going to disrespect people," she sighed as the guards watched him.

"By what honor have you earned the right to control me, you Terran filth?"

"I don't think I understand exactly what you want," she responded, mildly confused. "You act like you're not interested in the exercise, but when I talk about taking the privilege away you become defiant of that, too."

"I am sending a message to this facility. You will not control me unless you can defeat me. Until then, I will deny you everything you want from me, especially compliance."

"And by defeat, you mean in a fight?"

Vengence sat back in his seat and crossed his arms, glaring at her. The doctor finished writing on her pad and opened her mouth to speak when Vengence grabbed the bottle and turned it with the minus facing her.

"What is your work area, woman?" Vengence asked with his brows furrowed. "You breathe insecurity. What is your shame?"

She stared back, a bit shocked and confused. A moment passed as the two watched each other.

"I thought so." Vengence crushed the bottle with one hand and causing the top to shoot off into another corner of the room. "You are just as much a hypocrite as any other weakling on this planet."

Two security guards approached Vengence and attempted to usher him toward the door. When Vengence noticed them nearby, he stood up and shoved them both to the ground, scaring the patients.

"There is only one Terran I have met who I find worthy of a passing glance from me, and I excruciatingly admit it to be this imp!" Vengence shouted, gesturing to Stupor. "By comparison, that is pathetic! The rest of you are garbage!"

Vengence then walked out of the building door, pushing the two guards down again as they managed to get back to their feet.

The guards got up yet again and ran out of the silent room in pursuit. Dr. Perez stared at the crushed bottle while the patients looked around at each other awkwardly.

"You totally can't say we're not friends now!" Stupor proudly exclaimed, breaking the silence.

***

After the therapy session ended, Stupor took his time walking back to the living quarters. He gazed up at the starless sky and sauntered across the grass near the common room. An invisible orchestra of crickets could be heard playing their theme across the growth. A circle of silence followed Stupor as he stepped, blinding his eyes without deafening his ears.

I don't want Vengence to leave, he thought to himself. *We have a bond of friendship I haven't felt in anyone since Jörg. Not that Jörg isn't a great friend, but it's nice to have more than one person to talk to. And someone that can respond in the same language.*

Suddenly, he stood before Dr. Goodrich.

“Hi there, doctor! What a surprise!” Stupor greeted. “I thought you were gone for the day.”

“I was, but I decided to come back in to take some paperwork home that I forgot,” the doctor replied. “I’m glad I ran into you; I wanted to talk for a moment.”

“Oh?”

Dr. Goodrich put his hands into his pockets and glanced around him to make sure no one was near. “About the comment you made earlier about my wife,” he began. “I’m not having marriage issues with her, as you probably inferred from the state of my desk this morning. She is dying and I’ve been having a hard time dealing with that.”

Stupor was immediately socked by guilt as his heat sank into his stomach like a rock in a calm pond. “Oh… I, uh…” he started.

“No, wait,” Dr. Goodrich continued, cutting him off. “Despite the facts, you made a very good point and I do respect it. My emotions have been clouding my logic lately and people have noticed it affecting my work. They’ve suggested that I take some time off. I suppose I simply needed a proverbial bloody nose in order to open my eyes and see it for myself. I’m glad I ran into you and wanted to thank you for that much.

“Don’t get me wrong, I still strongly suspect that you are feigning your mental illness and exploiting the tax dollars of many hard-working citizens and I am fully intent on continuing my case against you. But your childish behavior does deserve an amount of merit, which I'll definitely keep in mind.

"I left today to go spend some much needed time with my wife. It hurts me to see her dying, but it hurts her more if I'm not there."

"I'm really sorry," Stupor apologized, upset with himself. "Really, I was just trying to—"

"Don't worry," Dr. Goodrich cut him off yet again. "You couldn't have known. Just consider us even. You should probably get going to your cell now."

Stupor sheepishly nodded and quietly moved past the doctor into the living quarters.

***

Lanzendorf sat sloppily on the couch in his apartment, watching television with the remote resting in an open hand. He lazily continued to wear his work slacks with an untucked white undershirt while around his face a five o'clock shadow grew. Still extremely upset over recent events, he flipped aimlessly through television channels, relying on the simple motions and constantly changing sounds to keep his mind and mood occupied.

When I get back, I swear I'll strip every privilege that kid has, he thought to himself, unable to shake Stupor's mask from his mind.

Suddenly, he noticed he could hear his cell phone buzzing from the dining room table.

"Damned things," he swore as he picked it

up. "It's not silent mode if I can still hear the stupid thing vibrating!" He flipped it open and frowned on sight of his text message. "I didn't sign up for these stupid joke texts! How do I keep receiving these?!" he ranted, clapping the phone shut. "I don't even feel like dealing with this crap right now!"

Before he set the phone down, he noticed a new voice mail on the front display. Sighing, he opened it back up and dialed into his mailbox as he examined the contents of his refrigerator.

"*First message: Friday at 5:57pm.* Testing, one... two. I'm Ralph. You asked me to get you coffee. I went to the break room and got it. Then I came back and you were suspended. So I'm calling you with updates like you wanted. I waited for you to come back, but then the coffee got old. I poured it in the trash but kept the cup in case someone else wanted coffee. The trash bag leaked and the coffee is in my trash can. I didn't know what to do with it so I put it in your office. I need a new trash can. Then I went home. Bye.

"*Next message: Saturday at 6:04pm.* Testing, one... two. I'm Ralph. I waited for you in my office. You didn't show up. I didn't know what to do, so I sat in my office for a while. I got bored and walked around. I asked some people if they wanted any coffee. After a while Mr. Bark told me not to talk to patients anymore. Then I had my lunch. I forgot my milk. I ate a piece of circle meat and a granola bar. Stupor asked for coffee."

Lanzendorf scowled.

"There was no coffee, so I waited. I didn't go home. Bye."

"*Next message: Sunday at 3:32am.* Testing, one... two. I'm Ralph. I had an accident. I don't want to talk about it. Bye.

"*Next message: Sunday at 7:46pm.* Testing, one... two. I'm Ralph. I waited for you in my office. You didn't show up. I didn't know what to do, so I sat in my office for a while. I got bored and walked around. I saw someone made coffee last night, so I got some. I gave my coffee to a weird guy in a mask. Then he asked for a copy of the passdown form."

Lanzendorf's eyes popped open on hearing this.

"The accident happened again. I got away from it, though. Then I gave the mask guy my passdown form. Everybody hurt my feelings and I ran home. I didn't make it home. I'm lost. Can you come get me? Bye."

Lanzendorf hung up the phone and stared at it, his mouth agape.

The passdown form?! he thought to himself, beginning to hyperventilate. *Why would B256 want the passdown form?! He's learning the security procedures? Why would he... Is he... Oh my god, C26!* Lanzendorf began to breathe heavily as he came to a horrible realization. *He-he isn't trying to get me fired! He's trying to escape with C26! I-I have to get there to stop him!*

Lanzendorf grabbed his keys and wallet as fast as he could and sped out the door for his car.

***

Stupor entered his cell and climbed up to his top bunk without even noticing Jörg laying in bed underneath him.

"Gute Nacht," he said as Stupor passed him.

"Have a good night, buddy," Stupor replied, crawling under his covers.

I really admire Vengence's desire to take charge of his life and poo on the rules. He knows exactly what he wants, Stupor thought to himself. *He'll do anything and everything to uphold his honor, it seems. He deserves to be happy, and I'd be selfish if I didn't try to help him leave just because I don't want him to.*

After he leaves, everything will probably go back to normal. Mr. Lanzendorf will also be back eventually, hating me more than ever... I'll be hanging with Jörg and playing checkers with Beeboo... Days will once again go by so fast I fail to notice anymore...

I suppose as bad as things are they could still be a lot worse. I could still have someone trying to kill me.

Chapter Thirteen

"Oh look, a field. It's so open and bright. What is this field? It represents freedom, I bet. The sun is shining!"

YOU HAVE NO IDEA WHAT YOU ARE DOING

"I'mma dance! I'm dancing! Blub, blub, blub..."

YOOSA GONNA DIE

"Bright lights on the horizon..."

LOVE THYSELF

"A celebration in another world... people are dancing and playing something that looks like a pan flute. It probably has a made up name, like flarjack."

DIEDIEDIEDIEDIEDIEDIEDIEDIE

It starts. Wake up!

***

Stupor jumped awake and noticed a hand holding a kitchen knife above his sternum. He felt consumed by an icy fright and froze as its finger poked straight through to his heart. He stared at the knife for what felt like eternity.

The knife abruptly plunged, headed directly for his chest. He knew in his head it was moving as quickly as the wielder could manage, yet it moved so slow in his perception.

He instinctively grabbed the wrist with one hand and threw it upward as hard as he could, banging it against the ceiling. The knife's wielder managed keep a grasp on the knife, but jumped off the bunk bed ladder in surprise.

Stupor jerked himself upright and looked down at his assailant only to see Jörg.

"Jörg...?" Stupor uttered, flabbergasted. "You attacked me?"

"Die Frau konnte nicht lösen Rätsel, so jetzt bin ich dran!" he said with a horrible smile on his face. "Sie sagen, die einfachste Lösung für ein Problem ist das beste, aber nicht mit dir, mein Freund. Jetzt wollen wir Sie Ihnen eröffnen und sehen, was diese Antworten sind..."

Stupor found himself unable to hear Jörg's words through the unbridled rage that welled within him.

"You're with the killer nurse, aren't you? You want me dead too, don't you?!" he shouted.

Jörg laughed heartily in response and pointed

the knife at him.

Stupor struggled for words, yet found himself unable to speak. An intense pressure built in his head like he had never felt before. His brain wrenched in pain, though his emotions couldn't have cared any less. As he drew in a deep breath, he felt his sense of choice slip away and his fury take full control.

Without another word, Stupor threw himself off of the bed toward Jörg, who responded by lifting the knife up to strike. Stupor's mask hit Jörg's hand again and the two crashed into the wall before crumpling to the ground.

The loud bang caused a few inmates to cry out in surprise, scared out of their sleep. They could be heard talking to each other as footsteps approached from afar.

Jörg raised his hand to swing the knife wildly, but Stupor was already on his feet and stomped his arm hard. As Jörg recoiled, Stupor gave two more hard stomps to his wrist. Jörg cried out in pain and dropped the knife.

Unable to control himself, Stupor jerked Jörg up from the floor, tearing his shirt, and threw him across the cell. He hit the cell door with a loud bang. Inmates shouted for guards as Stupor headbutted Jörg's face endlessly, sandwiching his head between Stupor's mask and the door. Jörg's consciousness was slipping away and blood began to gush from his forehead as it split wide open.

Three guards stormed into the cell, pulling Stupor and Jörg out to separate them.

"He attacked me with a knife!" Stupor cried out repeatedly. "Let me go, he's with the killer nurse! He's corrupted too!"

When the guards did not release him, Stupor wriggled free and backed away. "How long was it gonna take you guys to get here? How did you not even know he was going to kill me? You're supposed to be protecting me!" He continued to wail, not even waiting for them to answer. "Are you all on the same team or something? Nurses, patients! Why not security guards, too?"

"He's manic, we need to calm him down!" a guard said aloud as the three turned on Stupor and extracted their stun batons.

"*How dare you?! To protect life and property, what garbage!*" Stupor continued.

Familiar wicked thoughts flooded his head as the eyes on his mask began to glow brightly. The brightness engulfed the guards and washed the hall with beams of saffron. Stupor clutched his pounding head and braced himself.

"*All I ever wanted was a good life! I got stuck with a shitty life!*" Stupor shouted as the guards quaked before his horror. His voice resonated in their minds, his accusations imprinting on their souls. "*And now I don't even get to have a life?! You honorless cowards disgust me!*" Stupor continued.

The guards watched in abject terror, finding themselves unable to move. Their legs stopped responding as their minds became polluted with a paralyzing fright. The patients began to cry out in unintelligible fear as the air around everyone began to blacken. The watched on until all they could see were each other and Stupor, his mask's eyes sending their fight or flight senses haywire.

"C-call for... for backup!" one guard cried.

"I'm... scared!" whimpered another.

Stupor, unable to restrain himself, lunged at the guards and delivered harsh chops to two of their throats followed by a spinning kick to the face of the third. They all landed hard and two of them scrambled ran away, screaming. One body remained crumpled on the floor.

"Das ist die Antwort! Das ist die Antwort!" exclaimed a groggy Jörg as tears streamed down his ecstatic, smiling face.

Stupor brutally punted Jörg's head as hard as he could, instantaneously knocking him out. He then moved over to the remaining guard who had by now broken into tears, ripping the key card off his lanyard.

"If I stay here, I'm dead!" Stupor shouted at him, displaying the key.

"B256 is out and he's gone berserk! Requesting immediate backup to the living quarters upper floor!" Stupor heard the guard's radio buzz.

Suddenly, Stupor felt extremely light-headed as his mask's eyes stopped glowing and staggered to a wall to prop himself up. Regaining himself, he looked over his shoulder confusedly to see the guard getting up from the floor and picking up his stun baton, knees shaking. He looked about the area with a horrid sense of dread followed by urgency.

Oh, crap! Uh... plan B, I guess! Stupor thought to himself and ran to Vengence's cell. Vengence stared out the window with wide, doubting eyes.

"No time to talk, buddy!" Stupor quickly said to him. "I've changed my mind; we're escaping together right now, and I know exactly how to do it!"

Stupor swiped his key through Vengence's cell door lock, freeing him. He calmly stepped out and watched Stupor suspiciously, cracking his knuckles.

"Stay here and start the riot!" Stupor said to him prior to running down the stairs.

Stupor exited the building and looked at a locked plastic box labeled 'Emergency Override' immediately next to the door. He gave the box a couple hard kicks, breaking it open and revealing a card swiper inside. Stupor quickly swiped the card and ran back into the building. He looked over his shoulder as he went in the door and saw several guards running toward him.

Just as he reached Vengence, all the cell doors unlocked and swung open. Frightened inmates stumbled out into the hallway, looking around confusedly.

Paul, ran full force out of his cell all the while screaming, "I knew it! I knew it!"

Beeboo strayed too close to Vengence, who smugly picked him up and hurled him into the crowd of inmates.

"No Beeboo again!" Beeboo cried as several people were knocked down by his weight.

The commotion along with Stupor's actions worked the inmates into a frenzied herd of cattle, obstructing any guards that entered the hallway behind Stupor and Vengence.

"To Lanzendorf's office, come on!" Stupor shouted to Vengence before running ahead.

Vengence, having little choice, followed after him. As he rounded the corner, Stupor ran back upstairs past him.

"Get the guards, get the guards!" he cried.

Four guards came upstairs with their stun batons in hand. As Vengence prepared to fight them, he heard a crash as a patient fell past him and down the stairs, knocking the four guards over.

"Never mind, I took care of them all," Stupor declared, running past Vengence yet again and grabbing a couple stun batons as he hopped over the guards.

Vengence growled impatiently and followed Stupor, exiting the building. The four guards followed in pursuit as three more approached the barons. The two stared down the army of seven, who proceeded to surround them.

"Don't do this! We don't want to fight you guys!" Stupor attempted to reason.

"Put down those stun batons, B256!" a guard commanded.

"You have a huge riot going on upstairs. Are you sure you want to waste your time on the two of us?" Stupor argued, pointing in the direction of the commotion.

After thinking for a bit, three guards left for the living quarters building while the remaining four went after Stupor and Vengence.

Vengence grabbed a guard and slammed him into a second with as much force as he could muster while Stupor danced around the last two, zapping them with the stun batons. When they weren't paying any attention, Vengence delivered hard punches to their backs, knocking them to the ground.

The guards remained writhing on the ground and the two continued their way to the security building with Vengence effortlessly moving faster than Stupor.

"How does a big guy like you move so fast?" Stupor asked him in surprise.

"Shut up!" he responded as he approached Lanzendorf's office window, which was covered by a tremendous blue tarp. "I hate that we are doing the exact plan I spoke against yesterday. This is only because I have no choice!"

Vengence jumped in through the window, knocking down the tarp in the process. He was shortly followed by Stupor.

"Break the cameras for me, please? So I don't get seen?" Stupor asked.

Vengence balked at the idea, but snatched down any cameras he passed as the two worked their way down the hall and into the CCTV room.

The guard lazily sitting at the chair jumped and gave Vengence a very frightened look before being smacked unconscious by the force of his open hand.

"Vengence! It's working!" Stupor said while excitedly pointing at the monitors.

Vengence followed Stupor's finger and saw many guards rushing from their posts into the riot at the living quarters. A dissatisfied scowl washed across his face.

"Now we just have to shut these cameras off," Stupor commented. "If only there were some kind of virus I could put on here to keep them from being turned back–"

Before Stupor could finish, Vengence ripped the computer off of the counter, scattering the monitors across the floor. He then slammed the computer on the floor and smashed his two balled-up fists through it, completely mangling it.

"I suppose that works too," Stupor resigned, mildly disappointed.

Officer Herald was seen sitting behind the counter in the check-in room and nearly fell out of his chair once Stupor and Vengence entered.

"You have a choice to make, Officer Herald," Stupor informed him. "Your job status won't change at all regardless of what you decide."

Herald immediately waved them through, the barons passing behind him and into the inmate storage. He cringed in fright as Vengence passed. Once they left the room, Herald immediately got up and left through the opposing door.

Vengence quickly rooted through the plastic tubs until he found one labeled 'C26'. Reaching inside, he pulled out some bizarre clothes and a very strange helmet.

As Vengence extracted his plastic container, he saw that Stupor had dutifully stacked other miscellaneous tubs to form a wall behind which he couldn't be seen.

"What in the world are you doing?" he asked impatiently.

"I'm changing into my normal clothes. Don't peek!" replied Stupor from behind the makeshift wall.

On finishing, Stupor kicked over the tubs and thrust his arms into the air in a dramatic fashion. He happily sported his old striped shirt and jeans. Along with these clothes he also wore a dark gray winter coat, fastened around his neck like a cape. He noticed Vengence ignoring him and completely naked.

"Holy crap man, hurry up and get decent!" he cried, covering his eyes as Vengence rolled his.

In mere moments, Vengence was dressed and fastened his helmet over his head. The helmet had a small antenna on one side and a darkly tinted visor that stopped just under the tip of his nose. Hanging from the helmet was a chin strap.

Over his chest he wore an odd black vest, decorated with ports and a few visible wires. Underneath were a pair of black shorts and on his feet were flat-footed rubber boots, stopping halfway up his thighs.

"What's that thing?" Stupor asked, pointing at his curious headwear.

"This is a tracker helmet, now stop wasting... Why are you wearing your coat in that ridiculous manner?"

"I'm so glad you asked!" Stupor gleamed with pride. "'tis both a coat and a cape! Therefore, 'tis my cope! It's like a coat, but so much more!"

Vengence gave Stupor a critical stare before a two guards with an orderly suddenly burst into the room from behind. Before Vengence could react, two guards hit him with their stun batons while an orderly rammed a tranquilizer needle into his side and began to inject.

"Vengence, no!" Stupor cried as he grabbed a stun baton and threw it at the guards.

The orderly was hit in the leg, causing him to buckle and release the syringe. Vengence ripped the needle out and thrashed violently, knocking the guards into the shelves.

"I... hate... tranquilizers!" Vengence roared as he knocked patients' tubs off of the shelves and slammed more of them on top of the guards. In moments, they were all completely buried.

"It, uh... takes quite a bit to knock you down, yes?" Stupor asked.

"This will debilitate me, but as long as I keep my adrenaline up I should be fine for a while," Vengence answered while walking past Stupor to another door. "The warehouse is here, correct?"

Stupor nodded his head and the two moved through with Vengence taking point. As they entered the warehouse, they were ambushed by two more guards. One struck Vengence with a syringe and squeezed its contents into his body before being swatted away. Stupor meanwhile grabbed the second guard's arm with both hands and bent it upwards, pushing him away and into a shelf. Stupor backed away and braced himself for a counterattack.

Suddenly, he felt himself thrown forward as Vengence shoved him into the guard, knocking him over and stunning the guard. Vengence then picked up the guard and threw him into the patient belongings room while the first guard watched in terror.

"Don't use me like a weapon, man!" Stupor complained as the two stepped outside through the employee exit. "It objectifies me."

The cloudy night sky greeted them as a refreshing breeze ticked Stupor's skin. Vengence appeared dazed and dropped down to one knee. Noticing this, Stupor tapped him repeatedly on his shoulder to get his attention.

"Vengence!" he called to him. "Don't fail on me now! Freedom is almost ours! Vengence!"

Vengence quickly grabbed Stupor by his shirt and jerked him close.

"That... is not... my name..." he said sternly with a foggy expression.

Suddenly there was a flash of light from in front of Stupor. He looked over quickly to see something he could only describe as a humanoid robot.

The robot had a somewhat thin frame and appeared to incorporate unbelievably advanced technology. Its body and limbs were blackened while its hands, feet, and head were a lustrous silver.

On its head was a single red eye that moved from side to side, presumably scanning the area. After a brief moment, the eye rested squarely on Stupor. The robot took a step forward and held its hand out authoritatively.

"Baron Von Stupor, you are not permitted to leave the asylum," it said to him. Its voice was monotone and carried a light static.

"Those things... again?" exclaimed Vengence hazily.

"Wait, you can see them too? Oh man, what a relief!" Stupor exclaimed in utter surprise. "I was starting to think–wait, how do they know my name?"

"Return to the asylum or I will be required to use force," it coldly instructed.

"What the heck are you?" Stupor asked.

Suddenly, there was yet another flash of light and the robot was hit with a flying kick from a second, identical robot. The first was slammed to the ground and slid a short distance, emitting sparks against the pavement.

The second robot turned to Stupor and said to him, "Baron Von Stupor, you must escape the asylum. I will help."

"I don't... know how to feel about this..." Stupor uttered, now utterly confused.

As the first robot jumped back to its feet, there were several more flashes of light. Before long, Stupor found the entire parking lot flooded with perfectly identical robots in combat with each other. They all appeared to be using very advanced martial arts. Torn limbs and various miscellaneous parts found themselves scattered across the ground as more robots appeared in the lot to replace their fallen allies.

All Stupor and Vengence could do was sit and watch as the devastation continued. Robots teleported in an endless cycle like angry, warring bees. Stupor nervously looked over his shoulder and saw two security guards standing outside the warehouse, observing the chaos with jaws hung open.

Stupor then noticed a light emerging from the access road on the other side of the melee.

Oh god, he thought. *Those must be headlights! Is it the police? This is getting worse and worse!*

As the light came closer and got brighter, the fighting robots stopped in unison, directing their attention toward it. They then proceeded to scramble, picking up evidence of their fallen and teleporting away in flashes of light. It was all of ten seconds before they had disappeared without a trace.

"Vengence, we have to keep moving!" Stupor shouted as Vengence groggily rose to his feet.

Stupor feebly attempted to support Vengence as the two hobbled toward the gate. Before they got anywhere close, a car came bursting through and skidded to a halt. Turning off, Lanzendorf quickly jumped out of it and stared at Stupor with bulging eyes.

"I knew it!" he exclaimed hysterically while jabbing an angry finger at Stupor. "You were trying to escape the whole damn time!"

"Oh, thank goodness!" Stupor said, feeling brighter. "It's only Mr. Lanzendorf. Vengence, let's get out of here!"

"Over my dead body! You thought you were so slick," Lanzendorf taunted, a victorious smile on his face. "You had everything planned from the very beginning, didn't you?"

"What are you talking about?"

"From the moment C26 got into my asylum, you saw an opportunity to get out! You weren't trying to get me fired at all!"

"Actually, I only wanted to help Vengence escape at first, but then I changed my mind. But hey, can I go now? I'm in a hurry, but we can get a coffee sometime if you–"

"Shut the hell up! Your grand scheme ends here, you little shit! As long as I'm around, you'll never get out! Never... ever!"

Vengence, impatient, staggered over to the disheveled man. Lanzendorf coolly watched him approach feebly with his fists tightly clenched. He slowly raised his hand to swing, but was quickly pushed away by Lanzendorf. Before he could catch himself, Lanzendorf shot a hard straight punch to his jaw, toppling him over.

Vengence crashed to the ground and angrily looked up at Lanzendorf, struggling to maintain his vision.

The two nearby guards began to approach, but Lanzendorf pointed them back to the door.

"You've already been caught trying to escape, you know," Lanzendorf said to Stupor with a smug grin. "The board of directors will believe almost anything I tell them now. They'll even believe you came at me with a knife!"

"But I don't even have one!" Stupor shot back.

"They won't know that. They'll believe how I had to wrestle it out of your hands. They'll believe how you continued to fight back. They'll believe that you even put up a really good fight, and that it took every ounce of my strength to bring you two back in. They'll believe that I had to wrestle with you out here for a good twenty or thirty minutes before I could subdue you. They'll even believe that ultimately I had to knock you the hell out before you stopped resisting."

The two stared at each other as Lanzendorf took off his hoodie and threw it down on the pavement. Stupor released a sigh and shrugged his shoulders.

"It seems you know exactly what you want," Stupor said forlornly. "For our freedom, I must oblige."

Stupor took in a few breaths and assumed a silly fighting stance. He stood, his legs slightly bent and his arms turned up at ninety degree angles, his hands opened wide.

"I'm not going to hold back this time!" he warned. "Come at me if you dare!"

Lanzendorf fearlessly smiled and charged at Stupor, happily engaging him in a battle of fate.

Chapter Fourteen

Lanzendorf immediately threw a hard right at Stupor, who caught it under his right arm and twirled around it, stopping behind him. Stupor then used Lanzendorf's momentum to give him a hard push. Lanzendorf stumbled a few steps and glared at Stupor from over his shoulder.

Lanzendorf then turned around and lead in with a low right kick. Stupor quickly caught Lanzendorf's leg with his own, wrapping the two around each other. Before Lanzendorf could react, Stupor gave his leg a loud, open-handed slap. Lanzendorf recoiled back, stumbling once more as he freed his leg. Stupor hopped back to open some distance and taunted Lanzendorf by pointing his finger at him.

Lanzendorf angrily rushed Stupor, throwing many quick punches in rapid succession. Stupor was unable to catch any and instead worked on deflecting them the best he could. Once he was able to find an opening, Lanzendorf grabbed Stupor's arm and twisted it around his back.

As Stupor resisted his arm being wrenched, Lanzendorf took the opportunity to headbutt Stupor in the back of his head. After a couple blows, Stupor turned his head and Lanzendorf accidentally butted the broad side of his mask's horn.

With Lanzendorf stunned, Stupor continued thrusting his head back, hitting Lanzendorf twice with his horn's broad side. As Lanzendorf's grip became more awkward, Stupor was able to finally wriggle his arm free.

Lanzendorf moved to step in and was met with two quick jabs in the mouth from Stupor. Lanzendorf closed his eyes, stunned yet again. As soon as he regained sight, Stupor landed a fierce roundhouse kick on Lanzendorf's jaw. The force knocked him completely off balance and to the ground. Lanzendorf shook his head and looked up at Stupor, who was staring down at him.

"What kind of a person thrives on the misery and oppression of others?" Stupor asked him. "As strong as you are, Lanzendorf, the way you abuse your strength just shows how weak of heart you really are."

"What the hell do you know about strength?" he snapped back as he rose to his feet. "You're just some nut job in a stupid mask, doomed to rot here under my rule!"

Stupor raised his finger to argue, but noticed Lanzendorf fiddling with his pants leg as he got up. Stupor recognized a blade in his hand. His stomach fluttered wildly as Lanzendorf charged once more.

Stupor backpedaled, desperately dodging the madman's frantic swinging and stabbing. The two remained so focused on each other that Stupor didn't notice the curb of the parking lot island approaching him. He tripped on the curb, which in turn tripped Lanzendorf, and the two tumbled into the soft grass. Lanzendorf landed on top of Stupor as Stupor grabbed his knife-wielding hand. The two proceeded to roll around in the grass, Lanzendorf struggling to wrestle his hand free.

Lanzendorf eventually managed to roll over onto Stupor and straddle him. He overpowered Stupor's grip and wrenched his hand free, raising his blade to Stupor's throat. Stupor stared back, completely defenseless. He felt his emotions rise, heralding dread.

"Again, patient B256," he hissed. "What do you know about strength?" he asked him with a grin of satisfaction. "You don't know a goddamn thing."

Lanzendorf pulled the blade back and gave Stupor's throat a thrust from its pommel. Stupor recoiled and began coughing uncontrollably.

Lanzendorf took this opportunity to grab his head by his mask's horns and slam it in the dirt repeatedly. With each successful impact, Stupor's movements became weaker and weaker until he completely lost consciousness.

Lanzendorf collapsed on top of him, catching his breath. His heart pounded with exhaustion as he gave a quick look over his shoulder. Vengence remained on the ground, glaring at him with half-closed eyes. He shakily stood back up and returned his knife to its sheath before looking through his shaking hands at Stupor's crumpled body.

"No one escapes from my asylum, you prick," Lanzendorf said as the two nearby security guards approached him.

"Should we... take them in, sir?" one guard asked Lanzendorf.

"Not just yet," he replied, staring at Stupor. "There's just one thing I want to know first. I've always wondered what's under this stupid mask."

Lanzendorf reached down and attempted to lift the mask, but Stupor's head seemed to move with it as if it were attached. Lanzendorf gestured to the guards for assistance. They obediently held Stupor's head down as Lanzendorf struggled with the mask. After a great effort, Stupor's face began to show when suddenly a tremendous beam of violet energy shot out from it. It violently surged forth and into the sky, missing Lanzendorf's face by a hair.

The three men stared in horror as the energy swirled onward, eradicating the tops of several trees in its path. With the explosion, they could hear sounds of people shrieking and children crying from underneath the mask.

They simultaneously let go of Stupor and fell backward, utterly horrified. The mask snapped back into place before silence returned.

Stupor stirred as he regained consciousness. With nary a word nor moment's hesitation, the guards shot to their feet and ran for the building, abandoning Lanzendorf. Stupor sat upright and glared at him.

"You attacked me with a knife..." he uttered, his rage growing. "You honorless pig!"

The eyes on his mask glowed as he rose to his feet. Lanzendorf face turned a sick pale as Stupor took a feral stance.

"You can't see at all, can you?" Stupor asked, his rage boiling over while Lanzendorf quailed in uncontrollable fright. "You can't see past the tip of your crooked nose!"

Lanzendorf scrambled to his feet and tried to run away, but was quickly pounced on by Stupor. He whipped around and looked straight into the glowing eyes of Stupor's mask. The air around them was engulfed in darkness, though Stupor remained as clear as a cloudless sky.

Stupor drew in a breath and roared as hard as he could muster, plunging fear straight into the core of Lanzendorf's soul. Lanzendorf wailed in terror and fled once more, tears streaming down his cheeks. Stupor dropped to his knees, clutching his head as he began to calm down.

Vengence hazily observed as Stupor's mask ceased its glowing and visibility returned to the parking lot.

To clear his mind, Stupor lightly smacked the side of his head a few times prior to surveying the area. Seeing Vengence watching him, he quickly scurried over to help him up.

"We're only home free if we make it into hiding, buddy!" Stupor encouraged. "Let's go!"

Vengence wobbled to his feet and staggered with Stupor into the woods, nervously eyeing the trees whose branches were utterly mangled by the evil beam.

***

Lanzendorf stepped into the restroom of the security building and looked at his swelling lip in the mirror with disgust. His eyes were red and puffy from crying and the side of his head was developing a welt from Stupor's kick. He could still feel his heart pounding as adrenaline raced throughout his body. His hands shook beyond control.

"Uh, sir?" asked a guard that followed him in. "About what happened outside..."

"Absolutely nothing happened," Lanzendorf quickly responded.

"But that mask..."

"Nothing happened," Lanzendorf repeated, turning around to face him. "Do you know why? Write about it in your shift report and see how it flies with management."

"But what was that? What did it all mean?"

"I don't know, but the best thing we can do is forget about it. Pretend it never happened."

"What about the escaped patients?"

Lanzendorf stared at the guard through the mirror as he imagined the various consequences of the night's events.

They disgraced this entire facility, he thought to himself. *I ran this empire perfectly for five years. That kid waited this entire time for the perfect opportunity to escape and did it. Once he had the right cards, it only took him just over a week. He actually beat me. All I can do now is try to clean up this mess the best I can.*

"Sir?" the guard persisted, snapping him out of his thousand yard stare. "What are we going to do about the escaped patients?"

"I'll take care of tonight's incident report," Lanzendorf responded calmly.

"Do you want me to call the police?"

"No. I'll take care of it."

The guard nodded and turned to leave the restroom. Lanzendorf firmly grabbed him by the shoulder and turned him back around.

"Don't forget," Lanzendorf reminded him. "Nothing happened out there with B256. If you think something did, it's best to just wash away the thought. Otherwise you might be in here as a patient yourself."

"Understood," the guard agreed, nodding his head and leaving the restroom.

***

Stupor and Vengence continued to wander through the eerie woods, stumbling around trees and over rocks. The darkness was heavy and the ever dimming light of the asylum served as their only sense of direction.

"I think if we go straight we'll hit some road," Stupor commented. "I remember the driveway wraps around a ways."

"We must return to the woods if we see any light," Vengence replied as he dragged his feet. "The darkness of the woods is crucial until we are far enough away from the asylum."

After what seemed like endless blundering, Stupor tripped onto a flat surface. He reached down and examined it with his hand, feeling the texture of asphalt and road paint.

"This is the path to town!" Stupor exclaimed, pointing in an off direction without realizing that Vengence could not properly see him. "We need to go that way to get more towards civilization."

Noting his folly, he tugged at Vengence's arm to guide him. Vengence grumpily snatched his arm away and started down the road.

The two walked in total silence for a while, progressing toward a junction lit by a streetlamp surrounded by complete darkness. Along the way they passed a road Stupor recognized as heading back toward the asylum.

"Now I'm quite confident that this road goes into town!" Stupor happily announced.

"Be quiet," Vengence commanded him. "We need to stay alert. The tranquilizer is wearing off, but I am not at my full strength yet."

Upon reaching the junction, they could see the road fork in two directions. If they turned to their left they would only find another road that continued into the darkness. Down their current path they saw a blooming urban area rife with light yet devoid of life.

Upon getting closer to the lit area, Vengence strayed away from the road and continued along the edge of the woods behind a building.

"Wait! Where are you going?" Stupor asked, pursuing him.

"I am going to set up a refuge in this alley between the buildings," Vengence answered over his shoulder. "It has good cover and access to the woods if I need to make a sudden escape."

He stepped into the alley and looked around. The ground was paved and poorly maintained. He kicked a small chunk of road up and found some soft earth underneath. He then proceeded to pull up more pavement and dig out the dirt, slowly carving his way down.

"Why not hide in this dumpster?" Stupor suggested, pointing at a bin filled with trash. "It's a lot faster than digging out that pothole."

"I am above such filth," Vengence snapped back. "I will subject myself to the earth before Terran refuse."

Stupor curiously watched Vengence as he diligently carved out a hole big enough for him to fit in, scattering the scooped dirt all about the alley. Once the pothole was finished, Vengence rustled about in the dumpster and extracted a cardboard box.

"I am going to rest now. Leave me alone," Vengence told him coldly as he lowered himself into the pothole.

Stupor watched as he disappeared completely into the recesses of the hole, using his cardboard box as a roof.

I guess I get the dumpster, then, Stupor thought to himself, leisurely hopping into the heap of garbage and sliding the plastic door shut behind him.

Stupor found himself surprised by the lack of smell despite the surrounding trash. He explored around and noticed that most of the contents were metal scraps and mechanical parts.

This could be a whole lot worse, he thought to himself, feeling better.

Stupor leaned back and carefully rested his head on a garbage bag. Reflecting on things, he found himself feeling a strange combination of uncomfortable, yet excited.

***

"It was all over."

"Then it wasn't."

"Now it is."

"It's never over."

"Don't say that! This is only the beginning!"

"Every beginning has an end."

"Donkey Kong doesn't end!"

"……"

"CACTUS!"

click

Chapter Fifteen

Stupor awoke somewhat groggily to the sound of rustling cardboard. He excitedly got up and stuck his head out to see a helmetless Vengence crawling out of his pothole as the sun poked out from beyond the horizon.

"How was your sleep?" Stupor asked, resting his chin on crossed arms.

"Terrible, but tolerable," Vengence replied gruffly without looking at him. He stood up and lightly brushed himself off.

"You seemed to recognize those weird robots from last night," Stupor mentioned. "What were they?"

"I do not know. Their autonomy is incredibly advanced for my time as well. They have been hunting me every now and again for as long as I remember being in this time. I have fought a few of them in single combat in the before. They are quite formidable, yet very fragile."

"But if they're hunting you, then how would they know me and why did they fight over me going back to the asylum?"

"I know next to nothing about them except that they dislike attention," Vengence answered, turning to face Stupor. "I for one would love to know why they make orders of me and then turn on each other. They must apparently have some agenda for you as well, as you are the only other person I know that they have approached."

"They look really cool!"

"And they were likely built by a moron."

Stupor chuckled and clambered out of the dumpster, landing hard on his feet.

"So now that you're out, what are you gonna do?" he asked with his hands on his hips.

"My next immediate task is finding out how to get home. If I fell back in time, surely I can climb forward as well." Vengence then looked at Stupor critically and continued, "I suppose you are my only ally in this pitiful world of weaklings. This is a good place for a main base and I will welcome you to it for now. However, when you are no longer of use to me I will be severing our ties. I will not allow you to jeopardize my mission any more than I must. Besides, there is no telling exactly how much I may have impacted the future by allowing you to escape the asylum in the first place."

Stupor happily swung his arm in response and said, "Vengence, I have a feeling we'll be the best of friends!"

"For honor's sake, can you at least try to curb your contraction usage?" Vengence snapped in reply. "I lost our wager, but I feel like you are rubbing it in with your flippancy!"

Stupor stared at him for a moment and then gave him a quick OK gesture. Vengence scoffed back before sitting down with his back propped against a building.

"I guess I should go visit my family," Stupor mentioned after a moment of silence. "I have some money saved up from before I got arrested.

Maybe I can find a cheap bus ticket!"

"That sounds like a stupid idea."

"It probably is, but I really miss them! I like to think that maybe I can change their minds about me belonging in the asylum."

"That reminds me," Vengence said, standing up. "Last night I felt something very alien to me. As you were fighting the guards near your cell and again while you shouted at Lanzendorf, I felt fear."

Stupor looked at Vengence and shrugged his shoulders. "Everybody gets scared sometimes," he commented. "It's nothing to be ashamed about!"

"You do not understand. I am conditioned to be fearless. The fright I experienced did not feel natural. Does your mask have something to do with that?"

Stupor stared at him for a moment, rubbing one of the mask's horns. "Oh, this old thing? You needn't worry about it," he replied evasively. "'Tis a long story, involving gnomes and waffle irons. It's pretty raunchy!"

"I insist. I want to know about your mask. What is its significance to you? I remember in our battle you were very sensitive of it."

"Oh..." Stupor uttered, nervously drumming his fingers together. "So gnomes, they have this tendency to be unclean. It's pretty appalling, the things they do with their hands! They stick them in unsanitary places, like—"

Before Stupor could finish, Vengence dashed at him at a breakneck speed. He swiftly grabbed

Stupor by the neck and yanked his mask up. A horrid burst stream exploded from underneath, shooting straight up. Stupor flailed maniacally, futilely trying to escape Vengence's iron grasp. Vengence watched as the wicked surge pierced a cloud above, leaving a large swirling hole in the sky. After a few moments of hearing screaming people and crying children from under Stupor's mask, Vengence released it. The mask instantly snapped down and Stupor fell to the ground, breathing heavily.

"I doubt that is the work of dirty gnomes and waffle irons!" Vengence sharply declared. "If you want me to trust you, Stupor, you had better tell me about that mask!"

After catching his breath, Stupor stood up in an angry huff. "This is a bad, bad mask and I want nothing to do with it!" he shouted while angrily jabbing his finger at it. "And if you know what's good for you, then neither do you!"

Vengence suspiciously watched Stupor stomp back to the dumpster and climb in, slamming the door shut from inside.

***

That evening, Lanzendorf was called in to an emergency meeting with the board of directors. As he entered the room, they all seemed visibly distressed.

"Mr. Lanzendorf, there is a serious problem," Mr. Bark mentioned.

"I bet there is," Lanzendorf replied matter-of-factly. "I don't know why you're calling me back in here, unless it's perhaps to beg me to whip your security staff into the shape they were in before my untimely and undeserved suspension."

"That's not what we're discussing right now. Apparently there was another riot. Somehow the patients were released and left their rooms after lockdown. Afterwards, chaos. Pure and absolute chaos!"

"It appears nothing goes right when I'm not around," Lanzendorf said with his chest puffed out.

"Cut the crap, Bill," Mr. Jenkins cut in. "You were here last night, right? Were you here when those two patients escaped?"

"I didn't think the security staff could be so incompetent without my leadership," Lanzendorf mused, feigning ignorance. "Perhaps if Officer Abernathy were still here–"

"You were here last night!" Mr. Bark barked, raising his voice. "Stop dancing around it! B256 and C26 are missing and you are responsible!"

"How dare you accuse me of such a thing! What do you know about my whereabouts last night?"

"When I came in this morning, I noticed a whole lot of logged security policy violations from your computer's IP address," Sean cut in. "Either you were in your office outside allowed hours changing files in password protected areas of the network or someone else logged onto your machine and framed you."

"W-what?" Lanzendorf gasped, beginning to sweat bullets. "But..."

"B256 and C26's files all seem to indicate a healthy release," Mr. Bark told him. "This is an unauthorized motion, performed right from the computer in your office. Your staff seems to agree that you were indeed on the property last night. I hope you understand what this seems to imply."

Lanzendorf's mouth dropped open as the directors shot suspicious glares at him.

"You honestly suspect that I... I-I don't even have a motive!" he rattled, growing increasingly uneasy. "How do you even know for sure that they didn't receive a perfectly legitimate healthy release?!"

Dr. Goodrich pulled a manila folder out of a bag next to him and slapped it hard on the table.

"My files are all handwritten," he rebutted. "I only keep required information on my computer. The rest of my work is done with a traditional style. If a delusional boy and violent man were to be granted healthy release, my approval would be in this file that I lock with a key taken home with me every single night."

Lanzendorf looked at the directors, frantic and speechless. He then turned to Dr. Perez, who appeared slightly uncomfortable.

"Do you believe me, Dr. Perez? I'm sure you do!" Lanzendorf said to her assertively.

"No more blackmail. I've had enough of it," she said with a worried expression. "I may not be a model team leader, but the magnitude of your actions overshadows every dirty secret this facility has ever had."

"What are you talking about, Dr. Perez?" Mr. Bark asked, suddenly looking to her.

"I've been hiding a Vicodin addiction," she replied solemnly. "I've been feeding it by stealing pills from the facility. Mr. Lanzendorf found out some time ago and he's been blackmailing me since."

Mr. Bark looked at her, disappointed. The room went silent as Lanzendorf began to sweat bullets.

"I'd have gone into rehab, but I didn't want to risk losing my job," she reasoned. "I love it too much to chance that. I didn't want to lose the respect of my peers, either... so I chose to hide it. Next thing I knew, that viper Lanzendorf found out and used it against me.

"I don't care what happens at this point! This crap has gone on long enough. I love my job, but not enough to save his."

Another awkward silence fell over the room. Mr. Bark sat with his face buried in his hands while Dr. Perez lowered her eyes to the floor. Sean twiddled his thumbs awkwardly and Dr. Goodrich returned his file to his bag.

"I did not help those two patients escape," Lanzendorf said very slowly and angrily. "I hated them both. I did not help them escape."

"Then I suggest you start talking and tell me what happened or I'll have police here so fast it will make your head spin," Mr. Bark threatened.

The pressure in Lanzendorf's head became unbearable as he realized there was no other way out.

"They escaped," he cracked. "They escaped from my perfect asylum!"

"And you covered it up?"

"Yes, I did!" Lanzendorf declared, his head proudly held high. "This facility is perfect under my leadership! They tainted perfection! I wanted to remove the putrid stain of their victory from this place's history!"

"You committed several felonies in the name of perfect management?"

"I made this asylum what it is today and it will fall apart without me, don't you get it?!"

"All you've done was turn this asylum into a shitstorm and it all started with B256!" Mr. Bark snapped back furiously. "How can you be so selfish, arrogant, and self-righteous?!"

"You wanted great reviews and I delivered, old man! Don't you even dare talk to me about selfishness!"

Mr. Bark clutched his head in an attempt to ease the pounding.

"You need me here!" Lanzendorf continued. "Listen here, Bark. If you want this asylum to stand on two feet, you need my ways! Without that kid here, everything will be back to the way it was before, structured and peaceful."

"Mr. Lanzendorf," Mr. Bark began. "I will admit that most of my lenience has been due to your continued success with the asylum's reviews, but your actions as of late have been unethical, illegal, and borderline insanity."

"What are you trying to say?"

"I'm trying to say that I feel the best possible course of action would be to terminate your employment and sever your association with this facility in every way, shape, and form."

"Are you serious?!"

"I second," Dr. Perez said.

"I third," Sean added.

"Fourth," Dr. Goodrich chimed in.

A moment of silence passed and everyone looked to Mr. Jenkins. Suddenly realizing he was being stared at, he looked over at Lanzendorf's pleading expression.

"I, uh... I'm sorry, Bill," he said reluctantly, shrugging his shoulders. "I fifth."

"*You backstabbing son of a bitch!*" Lanzendorf swore aloud.

"Get out, Mr. Lanzendorf!" Mr. Bark sharply ordered. "We need to discuss this matter further and your input is no longer necessary. Have your office cleaned out by close of business tomorrow. If I see you here after, I will have you arrested on sight for trespassing."

Lanzendorf shot looks of hatred at the entire board of directors and stormed over to the door, stopping just short of it.

"By the way," he nastily said, leering over his shoulder. "Steve accepts bribes, too!"

Lanzendorf then left, slamming the wooden

door behind him as hard as he could. Outside the room, a painting could be heard crashing to the ground.

***

"Well, I'm heading out, Vengence," Stupor said to his ally as he lowered himself into his pothole. "I'll get a ticket for tomorrow morning and hang here the rest of the day. After that, well... I suppose that will be that. Thanks for everything!"

"Whatever," he replied callously. "I still feel you are throwing all of your work away by going home."

"Well, even if I don't stay there, I still want them to know that I'm okay. And just in case I come back to Friendly for some reason... you'll still be here, right?"

"This seems like a beneficial place to operate. I cannot promise it will stay that way."

"Well, in case I never see you again, good luck getting back home!"

"Hmph. I suppose I owe you some degree of thanks for your assistance with the escape as well. Appreciate it, as you will likely never receive such gratitude from me again."

Stupor smiled from underneath his mask and gave Vengence a big thumbs up.

"You're an awesome guy, Vengence!" he said. "Take care!"

"One more thing," Vengence mentioned to

him. "You tell me your real name and I will tell you mine."

Stupor looked at the ground for a moment and answered, "My name is Baron Von Stupor."

"That is what I thought."

Vengence carefully pulled his cardboard box over the pothole and lay down to rest. Stupor then chuckled and left for the bus station.

I'm no longer a part of the system... I'm me again, he thought to himself as he contentedly marched along the sidewalk.

Baron Von Stupor is his name, and this is his story.

"His story has only just begun."

Afterword
(Dennis)

If I were to visit myself in eleventh grade and tell myself that all of these funny scenarios we were imagining with Stupor and Vengence would evolve into a full length book, I'd think I was crazy. And yet, here we are a decade later and I am staring at my favorite personal project of my entire life: the birth of an epic saga.

With the creative input of some friends, I wrote this book. I took a little bit of my soul and placed it onto these pages. I made something that—to me—is living and breathing and yearning to meet other people. It wants to be heard, to be read, to be shared, to be loved.

I feel like developing Stupor has changed my life for the better in some ways. Many think that I use him as a self-insertion, when in fact they are only partially correct. While I definitely draw upon my past experiences for inspiration, Stupor is more an exaggeration of my own eccentricity. Seeing what he does and hearing what he says serves as a testament, and dare I say he even makes me quite proud of it. In a nutshell, Stupor's pride in his oddball ways makes me proud of my oddball ways, and in the closed-minded world we live in, we need all the support we can get!

Stupor in his own weird way is an inspiration to me, and for this reason I feel I owe it to myself and to Stupor to make sure his story is told. I'm proud of it not because I think it's a beautiful and entertaining story, but because this beautiful and entertaining story is proud of itself.

As an earnest thanks to everyone for showing their interest and support, I promise that this book will only be the beginning of Stupor's adventures. Oh yes, there is so much more to tell and I can't wait to tell it all. You will not be disappointed.

-Dennis L. Decker

Afterword

(Neil)

Nine years ago when the Baron Syndicate was conceived in its original form as a programming project in high school, I'd never have imagined it would get this far. It started as a grumpy old man and a boy in a mask who acted a little crazy. It has evolved a long ways over the years, always for the better.

Dennis and I have spent countless hours forming ideas and refining them, creating our characters and bringing them to life first in our imaginations, then on paper, then on a screen. It has in fact changed to a degree that it is in most respects not recognizable from what it started out with; mostly because our ideas early on were based on what we were interested in, even if it were copyrighted!

As it is I am both excited and nervous to see this passion of ours come into fruition so that we can share our love with everyone! Thank you to all who have read this story and to those who have supported all of our efforts!

Love,

Neil Miller

Special Thanks

William Lanza: If you can't tell from the book's dedication, Neil and I owe this man a ton of gratitude for things he never even realized he was doing. In high school, my programming class was given a simple project: to create a program that represents a product developed by a fictional company. We were allowed to select one partner, and being best buddies with Neil, the decision was obvious. This silly collaboration eventually led to the book you see before you. He deserves the most credit of them all.

Thuy Linh Decker: I suppose the general idea here is that I am a horrible person if I don't thank my wife somewhere in here. Linh, you did something which helped with something else... for some reason. And that thing you did had some kind of effect that couldn't be caused in any other way. Without it, something would assuredly be something else, which would have been far, far worse than what it is because of something you did. Thank you so much, Linh... for something!

Sean Ritzo: Super Editor Sean and his super editing skills were incredibly helpful during and after the book's development. Even though he's not officially a developer of the Baron Syndicate's plot, he has regardless been a great guy to bounce ideas off of whenever Neil is not available or when Neil and I have found some kind of disagreement. I couldn't have possibly picked a better devil's advocate than him.

Jessica Olsen: Jessica is very important for getting the Baron Syndicate on a significantly less impetuous path. After all this time coming up with great ideas, she asked the simple question, "Why aren't you showing how they met?" Such a simple thing to ask, and yet Neil and I wondered to ourselves why we hadn't been doing that all along. Thank you, Jessica, for giving the Baron Syndicate series a timeline that makes sense. Even if it made us feel a little dumb it was absolutely for the best.

Donna Neal: My mom yelled at me for not including her in the special thanks. I tried to explain, but she began beating me with a shovel. In between the clangs I was able to get part of my reason out, but then I lost consciousness. By the time I came to, I found myself tied to a chair in the middle of some field. After hobbling to the road, a drunk driver hit me. Thankfully they were going slow and I was struck in the back, the impact breaking the chair. In a few moments I was able to free myself. It was another few hours before I made it back home. Needless to say I won't be giving her any special thanks in this book.

Everyone else: When designing the different

asylum patients, I found it difficult to create a truly diverse cast of background characters on my own. Sure, I could throw darts at a board, but it seemed more natural to ask others what they might find interesting. It helped me immensely and made the asylum's populous feel more natural. A couple rare patients, a couple typical patients, and I owe thanks for all of them to the family and friends that offered their suggestions.

Additional thanks:

Uwe Daufenbach
English-to-German translator

Febrianto Pudi Utama (Pufutama)
Main cover illustrator

Biram Ba
Alternate cover illustrator

Paul Ritz Magtrayo
Alternate cover illustrator

Florence Min
Alternate cover illustrator

www.ingramcontent.com/pod-product-compliance
Lightning Source LLC
Chambersburg PA
CBHW021002120726
47905CB00009B/2809

* 9 7 8 0 9 9 1 5 5 9 5 1 0 *